LOBO RILER

Jason Manning

JASON MANNING

LOBO RILER

CHAPTER 1

Lobo Riler came down out of the high reaches of the Medicine Bow Mountains in April of the year 1867, riding a tall buckskin and towing a mule carrying packs of furs. Needing basic supplies such as flour, coffee, beans, black powder, plugs of lead, and a couple of pouches of smoking tobacco for his pipe, he left his remote cabin twice a year, shortly before and not long after the high country winters, to visit a town called Wild Horses located up on the North Platte hard by The Overland Trail.

He rode alone, and thinking about his destination reminded him that he was a lonely man. It had been five years since the passing of Quahneah, the slender, comely Cheyenne maiden who had lived with him for nearly twenty years. He knew then that those had been the best years of his life, and when "Morning Dew" had died in childbirth — the unborn child had not survived — he had thought that life, at least a life worth living, was over. He would have ended his life then but for the fact that he believed Quahneah was in the spirit world, with his child, and that to do so would have saddened them both beyond measure.

For the next few years he remained in melancholy isolation in the mountains, wanting nothing to do with anyone. Eventually, though, his need for essentials like lead and black powder had brought him down from the mountains. It was then that he had discovered Wild Horses — and his old friend Seth Topper.

He had also discovered the Regret, a brothel, and despite struggling with the feeling that he was betraying the memory of his beloved Quahneah, he had partaken of the pleasures of the flesh that such an establishment provided. This never had helped with the loneliness. If anything, being with a woman just made him feel even more alone when he returned to his mountain home. But there were needs a man had to attend to at least once in a while.

As had been the case for the past six years, he was accompanied by a blue-eyed wolf dog, the progeny of a three-legged wolf he had acquired from an enterprising old Arikaree Indian who peddled firewater of his own making to mountain men and Indians alike from a shack in the valley between the Medicine Bow range and the Sierra Madre. The Arikaree peddler had opined that the wolf was three-legged on account of getting caught in a trap and chewing the missing leg clean off in order to escape. The wolf hadn't gone back to his pack because in that condition it would no longer be welcome. Adult members of a pack had to pull their own weight or became a burden that wouldn't ordinarily be tolerated.

Because of that three-legged wolf, who had stuck with him the rest of its life, Riler had acquired the nickname Lobo, a name he never used to identify himself, but one by which he was widely known. That wolf had mated with a very large and ill-tempered Cheyenne camp dog to produce the animal that now traveled with him. As ill-tempered as the bitch had been, it had proven unable to withstand the amorous attentions of a wolf, even one short a leg. Riler's current companion was as large as his sire, with a black face and mane and shoulders that faded into gray further aft.

Riler was a lean man, wide in the shoulders and narrow in the hips. At six feet tall he loomed over most men. He had black hair, a thick and unruly head of hair that was salted with gray at the temples. His winter beard was black too, with a dusting of gray at the chin. Like the wolfdog, he was getting on in years. He had come west from Cincinnati in 1837 at the age of seventeen to escape the tragedy of both parents taken by the cholera epidemic that was sweeping across the continent at the time. The cholera chased him across the plains and reached the Pacific coast the following year.

Having sought sanctuary in the high country, where few people ventured in those days, Riler had never laid eyes on the Pacific coast. Taken in by mountain men — in particular one by the name of Seth Topper — he had learned the life and came to love it, for all its hardships. Looking back, he figured even the blackest cloud had a silver lining. But for the cholera he might have ended up spending his life working for a daily pittance in a slaughterhouse, like his father had done.

Emerging from the timbered foothills as dawn broke on the other side of the Medicine Bow range, the mountain man paused a moment to survey the majestic sweep of the broad valley that lay before him, just as morning light touched the snow-capped peaks of the cobalt-blue Sierra Madre to the west. Though he had seen it every day for twenty-five years, the beauty of the land he roamed was not lost on him even now. The valley below was greening up as the days began to warm and the snow to melt. It was still plenty cold though. The exhalations of man, horse and wolfdog were visible in the frosty air as Riler drank in the sight.

He wore a fringed deerskin shirt under an Indian blanket serape. He preferred the makeshift serape to a heavy coat of wool or hide because it afforded him more freedom of movement with his arms, which had saved his bacon a few times. His deerskin breeches were tucked into stovepipe boots. A wide-brimmed, low-crowned felt hat of nappy wool was on his head. A leather possibles bag was slung over his shoulder with a braided leather strap and hung on his left hip. The bag contained caps and paper cartridges for his 1852 Slanting Breech Sharps rifle, the.36 caliber Colt 1851 Navy Revolver stuck in his belt, his pipe and tobacco when he had some, and some flints for fire-starting.

He didn't linger long on the open slope. He was anxious to get to Wild Horses, to sell the furs his mule carried — some beaver plews that wouldn't bring much these days, and a few bearskins which *would* bring some coin, enough to buy supplies to last the summer — beans, coffee, salt, gunpowder and other necessities — with a little left over for a bottle or two of firewater and maybe an evening or two spent at Julie Regret's cathouse. So he pressed his legs against the responsive buckskin's flanks and the horse picked its surefooted way down the slope through the bluestem, last year's brittle brown stubs speckled with green new growth.

Riler hadn't gone far when, eyes narrowing, he checked the buckskin with an abrupt tug on the reins. He had ventured out onto the grassy flats far enough to see north past a rocky promontory jutting from the slope he had just come down. There was a smudge of black in the cloudless blue sky. He didn't think it was smoke — it was too concentrated and it wasn't trending eastward as smoke would be, moved by the gentle but persistent breeze coming down off the western range. Urging his horse into motion, he held it to a walk, his attention divided between the smudge and his more immediate surroundings. In these parts, anything out of the ordinary often meant trouble.

He had continued north a couple of miles when one of his sweeping looks to the west made him pull up on the reins again. There was something amiss in the sea of greenish-brown grass through which that western breeze was rippling. There seemed to be a gap in the surface of the grass, and he knew the valley well enough to know that it wasn't caused by a creek bed. He angled the buckskin in that direction and soon saw the wide swath of trampled grass. A large number of animals had run through here no more than two days ago, and by the way the stalks lay on the ground they had been heading south. Considering the breadth of the swath he decided it had to be sign left by a herd of buffalo on the movie. The bison tended to migrate north from their summer grazing grounds once winter was about over. He glanced right, at the dark smudge in the sky, and now he could tell it seemed

    Jason Manning

to be moving, revolving. Turning his horse that way and urging it into a lope, he stayed beside the swath and in a few minutes finally knew what he was looking at.

Buzzards. A lot of them, maybe as many as a hundred.

Riler had a pretty good idea what he was going to find well before he saw what had the attention of the buzzards. As he drew closer, he saw that some of the big black birds would swoop down, followed by a few more, and then more still. And then they would all rush back up into the sky. Buzzards weren't the only scavengers in these parts.

Atop a gentle swell of ground, he stopped his horse and stared down at the carnage. There had to be at least a hundred mounds of bloody black meat down there in the broad course of trampled grass — the skinned carcasses of buffaloes. Wolves and ravens were feasting and quarreling over them. The buzzards would sweep down on some unattended mounds, then take flight when challenged by the other scavengers.

Riler's bleak eyes swept the wooded slopes of the foothills to his right. He could envision the hunt quite clearly. The hide hunters had been there, concealed among the trunks of the aspen and pine near the bottom of the wooded slope. The buffalo herd would have been grazing about one hundred-and-fifty yards away when the hunter started shooting, once the sun rising above the rim of the Medicine Bow range behind them had illuminated their targets. The buffalo never saw them, didn't see the muzzle flashes when they turned their heads to look east, towards the sharp percussive snapping sound of probably two or three rifles dealing death with every shot.

The sharpshooters in the hide-hunting crew would aim for the lungs. It didn't surprise Riler that they could drop a hundred or more before the herd began to run which wouldn't have happened until enough of them sensed danger, or perhaps when a wounded animal attacked one of the others. The hunt was over then. The skinners would move, spike the dead buffalo through the nose and use teams of horses to peel the hide right off the carcasses. Except for a few choice cuts, including some tongues, taken by the crew to feed themselves for a while, the meat was left behind.

Riler looked down at the wolfdog. "Stay with me," he said. The wolfdog had been watching the scavenging wolves, but when his master spoke his ears swiveled and he looked up. Riler urged the buckskin forward at the lope. The wolfdog stayed by its left side. Over the years, horse and canine had become good friends. When Riler was about fifty yards from the nearest kills the scavengers began to take notice of him. As he rode closer, the wolves began to skulk away to more distant carcasses. This triggered some skirmishes among the lobos. The nearest ravens made loud croaking sounds, complaining about Riler's interruption of their gorging. They too moved to other carcasses, but they didn't go far. They weren't afraid of men. Men didn't hunt them. And many of them were heavily laden with buffalo meat and not inclined to take flight unless they had to.

One bunch of wolves didn't run off right away. There were three in this bunch, and the largest one, which Riler surmised was the pack leader, lowered its head and began snarling as the rider came within twenty-five yards of it. The wolfdog began growling and again Riler spoke to the wolfdog — "Stay with me." He reined in the buckskin and sat there, waiting with his hand on the converted Colt Navy stuck in his belt. He knew the wolves wouldn't attack him but there was always a chance the presence of the wolfdog would provoke an assault.

The pack leader produced an impressive threat display for a couple of minutes. All the while the wolfdog stood still, growling occasionally. Eventually the wolves turned and moved further away with occasional, sullen glances back at the rider who had intruded on their feast.

Riler rode along the eastern edge of the killing ground and soon found what he was looking for. A wagon had passed this way, and then turned and gone north. He followed the tracks. At the northern end of the killing ground the tracks of a second wagon, which had no doubt moved down the western flank of the killing ground, joined the first. These tracks moved north away from the slaughter and crisscrossed other tracks coming south. Riler realized those coming south and those going north were the same wagons, the former distinguishable from the latter because the wagons were considerably heavier after the harvesting of the buffalo hides.

　　　　　JASON MANNING

Soon the southbound tracks veered off to the east, in the direction of a rock outcropping — boulders that had long ago fallen from the rocky heights of the Medicine Bow range. Riler surmised that the wagons had been concealed behind those boulders, downwind of the herd. The crew knew what they were doing. The skinners, teamsters and cook had waited there until the hunters, probably accompanied by reloaders, did the killing a bit further south.

The slaughter didn't bother Riler. With his own eyes he had seen vast herds of bison and he was aware that buffalo coats had become fashionable back east, just as beaver hats had been in the past. In fact, a number of mountain men had turned to hunting bison for profit these days. He often came down out of the mountains to kill a buffalo, but not for money. Buffalo meat was preferred by himself and many of his fellow trappers to beef or venison. Just about every edible part of a buffalo was harvested. The Indians took the tongue and internal organs and considered them delicacies, but Riler had never been partial to either. Those, with bone and gristle, were just about the only parts of the kill he left behind. With all the strips of dried meat and pouches of pemmican he could make, a single buffalo would feed him for many weeks, while the hides provided parfleches and pouches for storage, as well as rugs and covers for the small cabin which he had called home for two decades.

Nor was he bothered by the fact that hide hunters were plying their trade so close to home. Such men rarely ventured into the high country, and that suited Riler, who had grown accustomed to living in isolation. He didn't like to be crowded. As far as he knew, no one else lived in his neck of the woods and he seldom saw sign of a human's passage anywhere near what he considered his private domain.

He rode north, following the tracks, estimated by the number of horses or pack animals accompanying the wagons that the hide hunting crew numbered around ten to twelve men, acknowledging the possibility that more than one man rode in a wagon. Reaching the northern end of the valley that afternoon, he expected the hide hunters to turn east, passing the northern tip of the Medicine Bow range and hitting The Overland Trail somewhere in the vicinity of Fort Laramie.

Instead, the hunters continued north. Up that way was South Pass, where many a settler had crossed the Divide in the past twenty years.

Riler didn't think the hide hunters planned on crossing the Divide. There was no reason to haul such a load over such a rigorous route. So there was only one reason for them to continue north. Their destination had to be the town of Wild Horses. That didn't bother him, either. Maybe some of them were former trappers, and he might know one or more of them. Maybe they would swap tall tales over a bottle of rotgut.

He calculated he would reach Wild Horses by mid-morning on the morrow.

The last thing he expected to find was trouble.

Chapter 2

Julie Regret woke with the dawn, as was her custom. She had her bed placed so that the rising sun came through the thin curtains covering the room's single window and lit up the bed. The house was usually quiet at daybreak after nights that were often long and rowdy, and such was the case this morning.

She lay there a moment, staring up at the ceiling, sliding a hand over the rumpled sheet to the other side of the bed even though she knew Moke wasn't there. Moke Regret had had a lot of faults, but she missed him anyway — missed him terribly, even after all this time. Her husband for a quarter of a century, Moke had broken his neck falling off a skittish horse. But he hadn't left her empty-handed — she had inherited this bordello a stone's throw away from The Overland Trail. Locals, along with teamsters, scouts, soldiers and Overland Stage Company drivers who plied the trail, called it simply the Regret.

Dwelling on Moke made her throw aside the heavy quilts that kept her reasonably warm during the cold high country nights. The longer she stayed in bed the more she thought of her dead husband. Rising, she saw her reflection in the cracked and smoky glass of the freestanding mirror in the corner. That didn't help her mood any.

She had once been a slender, pretty girl with lustrous brown curls. Her ample breasts had noticeably succumbed to gravity and weren't as perky as they had been a dozen years ago, and she thought her hips were a bit thicker, too. Her hair was still black as a raven's wing but had lost some of its luster. She worked some scented pomatum into it and then brushed it fiercely, pulled it back into a tight ponytail which was held in place with two horn hair combs. Then she stood there, hands on hips, and looked at herself, trying to be generous in the self-appraisal. At least, she thought, her face was still pretty, with big eyes, full pouty lips and high cheekbones. And she still had all her teeth.

Wearing a linen chemise and baggy open-crotch drawers, she began to shiver from the cold. Pulling a quilt off the bed she wrapped it around her shoulders and held it at her throat as she walked down an L-shaped hall, past four closed doors. The girls usually slept as late as possible, and just how late that was depended on how soon the men showed up. Descending the narrow staircase, she glanced right, into the parlor, a large and reasonably well-furnished room that took up nearly half of the ground floor. It was there that a girl would entertain the men until one of them paid to take her upstairs for a poke.

At the bottom of the steps she turned left, through a door into the dining room, and from there into the kitchen in the back of the house. She stoked the fire in the stove's belly and put on some coffee to boil. Deciding that breakfast for the girls this morning would consists of corn bread left over from the day before, along with fried potatoes and sausage, she went out the back door and hurried to the smokehouse, returning a few minutes later with the sausages. The kitchen had warmed up a bit, so she shrugged off the quilt and draped it across one of the two ladderback chairs at a small round table. By then the coffee was hot enough and she poured herself a cup through a strain, and sat down in the other chair to drink it and reflect on her life. She usually tried not to, since it often led to her drinking too much gin as the day progressed. But this morning she couldn't help it. Maybe, she thought, it was because her dead husband had been the first thing on her mind.

     Jason Manning

She had met Moke Regrette in New Orleans — he had shortened his name when the maker of a list of those who qualified for a bounty of 1280 acres of choice Texas soil following the War for Texas Independence left off the last two letters. Moke had been an enlisted man in the New Orleans Grays and she a young hospital nurse. The Grays had gone west in 1835 to join the People's Army of Texas in the fight against the rule of Santa Anna's Mexico. Moke had been a handsome, charming, dashing young blade in those days, and Julie had fallen hopelessly in love with him at first sight. He made good his promise to marry her and bring her to Texas after the war. The day of the wedding had been the happiest day of Julie's life. She had been nearly seventeen and fully expected married life to be wonderful.

At first Moke tried to make a farm out of the land he had been given, but he wasn't much of a farmer. In the years that followed he went from one grand scheme to another. In the process he and his wife gradually moved west. Then Julie had a pair of difficult pregnancies, each of which ended in a miscarriage. Around that time Moke began sleeping with other women. She stuck with him anyway because she didn't see that she had any options.

Lady Luck finally smiled on Moke. They arrived in the little town of Wild Horses in 1859. The year before, Moke had spent the summer mining for gold along Little Dry Creek, a tributary of the South Platte. Though he regularly visited whores who had set up shop in the boomtown called Denver, he managed to come away with enough gold to build a big house in Wild Horses, which he initially planned to turn into a boarding house.

With the Oregon Trail beset by hostile Indians, emigrants began to depend on a more southern route discovered by an army engineer named Howard Stansbury — a route already well known to mountain men and which was eventually called the Overland Trail. When Ben Holladay secured a mail contract from the United States Post Office Department, his Overland Mail Company used this route. The quiet little town of Wild Horses became a stop on the company's route to South Pass. But since most pioneers came in wagons, and army details didn't rent rooms, Moke's boarding house failed to make him much of a profit. He rode to Denver and returned with two whores and turned the place into a cathouse. Considering her husband's lifelong affinity for women of easy virtue, Julie wasn't surprised. She just had to get used to Moke bedding other women under the same roof.

Moke died a year after opening the cathouse and Julie had run it ever since. By that time she felt as though she needed to provide for the prostitutes who lived there. She thought of them as her girls, because they *were* her responsibility, even though a couple had been older than she. They had numbered as many as six at one time. Now, though, there were only three.

Despite Moke's infidelity, Julie had not harbored any resentment towards the girls, all of whom her husband had poked numerous times. She hadn't blamed herself, either — Moke had always found her attractive and had made love to her until the very end. Nor did she blame him. That was just the way some men were. She had been made aware that other women who learned of the situation thought less of her because she remained with her philandering husband. But the truth was she had always loved Moke — and loved him still.

Julie heard the *clump-clump* of booted feet on the stairs and when she looked towards the kitchen door, she realized her eyes were brimming with tears. She swiped at them with the back of her hand and managed a smile as a tall, lean, black-haired man wearing a black sack coat and matching trousers, along with a gold silk vest over a white shirt closed at the collar with a string tie, appeared in the doorway.

"Good morning, Mr. Caulfield."

As long as they didn't keep everyone else in the house awake, the girls could have overnight guests past the hour of midnight, at which time the Regret officially stopped accepting clients. But it cost the man who stayed the night an extra dollar, so very few clients did so.

"Ah, there you are, Mrs. Regret. I smelled the coffee all the way upstairs, an aroma so heavenly it persuaded me to leave Rose's beguiling arms. May I join you?"

Julie rose and moved the quilt off the other chair, throwing it over the chair which she had previously occupied. "Of course," she replied, turning to the stove. She poured Caulfield a cup of coffee and brought

JASON MANNING

it to him; while he sipped the coffee she sat down in her chair again and pulled the quilt around her shoulders.

"Ah, black and strong enough to float a horseshoe," he said. "Just how I like it." Caulfield gazed admiringly at her for a moment. "Your husband was a lucky man, ma'am. Had I had the pleasure of knowing him before his passing I would surely have told him so. Regret — was he a Frenchman?"

"Cajun. And quite the charmer, was he." Wearing a melancholy smile, she brushed a stray tendril of hair off her forehead. "Handsome as the Devil, too. I was quite flattered by his attention. I wasn't exactly the prettiest flower in New Orleans, you see." Her mind followed the trail of her memories, and she murmured, "Though I thought I was at the time." Then laughed at herself softly, shaking her head.

"I believe you *must* have been the prettiest of them all, considering how lovely you are now."

"You're quite the charmer too, I see."

"I only speak the truth, ma'am. Is that the hint of a brogue I hear in your lilting voice? Scottish roots I would say."

"You have a good ear as well as a smooth tongue, Mr. Caulfield."

Caulfield tilted his head. "I bet you were a wildcat in bed. Perhaps still…?"

Taken aback, Julie studied him in silence for a moment. Eldon Caulfield was a handsome man. He was tall and slender, with wavy walnut-brown hair, a thick drooping mustache and glacial blue eyes, a suave and salacious man of about thirty years. She recalled him claiming to be a veteran of the recent War Between the States; that he had been a lieutenant serving under General John Buford in the 1st Cavalry Division at the Battle of Gettysburg. Coming west after the war ended, as so many others had done, he served as a deputy sheriff for a time in Baxter Springs, Kansas, the destination for many of the first cattle drives from Texas. But, harboring a dream of reaching the Continental Divide and the lands beyond it, he had quit law enforcement and traveled west. This had brought him to Wild Horses a few weeks ago. While he rented a bed from the Chinaman, he spent much of his time — and a fair amount of coin — at the Regret.

She wasn't offended by Caulfield's rather bold advances. He certainly wasn't the only patron of the cathouse who had expressed an interest in getting her into bed. Nor was she the least bit flattered. Of the Regret's three girls, only Rose Waldron was truly pretty. That didn't mean the other two didn't want for customers, however. Molly Mayne was skinny and plain-featured, while Ana Rosario was a plump but pleasant woman not much younger than Julie, and had a face scarred by a Kiowa brave who had kept her as a squaw for a few years. Molly and Ana got poked as many times as Rose because in this wild country there weren't so many women that men could be finicky when it came to choosing their 'horizontal refreshment'. So she didn't let compliments go to her head, and suggestive comments did not faze her.

"I'm sorry, Mr. Caulfield, but you'll have to be content with the girls." She said it pleasantly, with a smile, as she got up from the table. Shedding the quilt, she donned an apron and busied herself collecting the ingredients needed for cornbread — cornmeal, cooking fat and salt.

"I hope I didn't offend you," said Caulfield, looking worried.

She laughed softly as she picked up a bucket and moved to the back door. "Not at all."

He rose from the table and took hold of the bucket's bale. "Please, allow me."

She smiled, nodded, and let go of the bucket.

When he returned with the bucket full of water from the well out back, she began to make and roll the dough. Returning to the table, he sat and drank some more of his coffee. "You have a very nice place here, Mrs. Regret. You and your girls make a fellow feel right at home."

"I am happy you feel that way. How much longer do you aim to remain in Wild Horses?"

"Well, eventually, I do intend to proceed to South Pass. And once there I suppose I will continue on westward. I think I would like to lay eyes on the Pacific Ocean. Have you seen it, Mrs. Regret?"

She shook her head. "I imagine this is as far west as I will get. And after you've seen the ocean, then what might you do?"

"I'm not entirely sure. Perhaps I'll become a peace officer again. I had some experience doing that in Kansas last summer and it suited me. Or have I told you that already." He reached under his coat and brandished a Colt Army Revolver, which he placed on the table. "I'm fairly handy with this, by the way."

"Did you have to shoot anyone in Kansas, Mr. Caulfield?"

"No. Though I did use this end…" he tapped the butt of the pistol "…on the skulls of a few Texas cow pushers who got a little too rowdy for their own good."

Julie heard the shuffle of bare feet on the wooden floor and glanced over at the door just as Rose came through. She had on her crotchless drawers and her chemise was unfastened, exposing her pert young breasts as she leaned against the door frame, yawning and stretching. Julie wasn't sure if that stretch was genuine or by design, to show off a willowy young body that no doubt haunted many a man's sleep.

"Good morning, Miss Julie," murmured Rose, then looked at Caulfield with a breathless, wanton little smile. "And good morning, Mr. Caulfield," she purred.

"Morning, sweets," said Caulfield, grinning.

"Morning to you, Rose," replied Julie. "Coffee on the stove." She shaped the dough to prepare it for the skillet. "And button up your chemise, dear. The less they see, the more they want."

"It's nothing Mr. Caulfield hasn't seen already," said Rose, but she buttoned her chemise before pouring herself a cup of coffee. Then she turned, sipping from the cup while sliding a hand under her drawers to scratch.

"If you have an itch," said Caulfield, "I would be happy to scratch it."

"And you scratch my itches so well, Sir!" replied Rose, with a soft, lilting laugh.

Caulfield turned slightly in the chair and patted his lap. "Come sit with me, girl."

Rose didn't hesitate, nor did Caulfield pause before insinuating a hand under the chemise.

"Did you sleep well, Mr. Caulfield?" asked Rose.

"I did indeed. I was exhausted, thanks to you, and awoke refreshed and … would have wakened you in a way I suspect you'd have enjoyed, had I not been lured away by the aroma of Mrs. Regret's coffee."

Rose wiggled in his lap a little. "Well, we can always go back up to my room after breakfast if you like. Of course, Miss Julie will require another dollar."

Placing the cornbread batter in an iron skillet, Julie said, "Yes, she will, in addition to the dollar for staying overnight," and marveled at how naturally Rose manipulated men. Unlike Molly, who was jaded and indifferent when it came to men, or Ana, who accepted whatever was done to her in stoic silence, Rose genuinely craved the attention and never stopped soliciting more.

Keeping an arm wrapped round Rose's narrow waist, Caulfield checked the pocket of his vest. "I believe I may yet have two dollars," he said, and then put them on the table and gave Rose a squeeze. "I swear, girl, you are well on your way to making a pauper of me."

As she was carrying the skillet to the stove, Julie glanced out the kitchen's single window, a small one the offered a view to the south, the sea of grass with its gentle swell, and the towering peaks blue and hazy in the distance. But her gaze locked onto a small caravan heading straight for town. Placing the skillet on the top of the stove, she wiped her hands with the apron and went back to the window.

She counted two wagons and eleven men, two in each wagon and seven of them on horseback. Two of the latter were towing pack mules. The wagons were piled high with buffalo hides, and each was pulled by a six-mule hitch.

"Looks like a hide hunting crew rolling in," she told the others.

Rose jumped out of Caulfield's lap and came to the window. She began to count under her breath. "Looks like eleven men, Miss Julie!" she said.

Julie nodded, and glanced at Rose's face, noting the excitement there. She tried to remember if hide hunters had come through Wild Horses since Rose had come to the Regret. She didn't think so. It had been awhile since she had seen any. Most such crews plied their trade

     JASON MANNING

further east, where the largest herds grazed the plains. There had been reports of more Indian troubles out that way the past few years, due to the increased number of westbound emigrants in their wagon trains — and the increasing number of buffalo slaughtered by hide hunters. So maybe this crew had decided to hunt the herd that occupied the valley of the North Platte, between the Medicine Bow range and the Sierra Madre, thereby avoiding the traditional hunting grounds of the Arapaho and the Cheyenne.

"I suppose they'll go on down the trail to Fort Laramie," Julie murmured. "That's where they'll find traders likely willing to buy those hides. So they may not have a lot of hard money, Rose."

Rose grinned crookedly. "Whatever they have, let's get it." She turned and went back to Caulfield and whispered in his ear. They left the kitchen together and Julie heard them hastening up the stairs.

Julie stayed at the window a while longer, brows furrowed as she watched the hide hunters come closer. One benefit of being married to a man who had wandered from Louisiana to Wyoming in search of success was that she had seen all manner of men, from farmers to cowboys, soldiers and scouts, prospectors and lumberjacks, businessmen and traders, lawmen and the lawless. She had even met a few diehard mountain men. But in her book, none were as rough or as raucous as hide hunters.

She hurried upstairs to get dressed, and heard the squeak of bedsprings through the door to Rose's room. All of a sudden she was worried about her girls, with a passel of hardcase men riding into town. Wild Horses didn't have its own lawman, much less a jail. It was a community of barely thirty inhabitants. It didn't have a bank, or a school, or even a church yet. If those eleven men riding in were troublemakers, there weren't enough men in town to stand up to them.

Entering her room, Julie chided herself for fretting so. The hide hunters probably just wanted some whiskey and some women and then they would move on and no one would be the worse for it. She dressed hurriedly in a simple brown gingham dress, pulled on her brogans, and went back downstairs to get back to cooking.

CHAPTER 3

Riler woke before daybreak, when the eastern sky was turning from gray to pale blue and night was fleeing westward. The ground-hitched buckskin paused in its grazing to whicker softly when he moved. The wolf, which had slept curled up beside him during the cold night was nowhere to be seen. Riler didn't worry about him, assumed he was off hunting up his breakfast and that he would return soon — or catch up if Riler was on the move.

And he was eager to be on his way. He hadn't built a fire last night and didn't this morning, though he missed not having some coffee. But with winter about over, all sorts of people could be on the move in the valleys, and he didn't care to attract attention. With no coffee to linger over, he saddled the buckskin, rolled up his Indian blankets, tied them behind the hull and was mounted and moving north before the sun came up. By his estimate the town of Wild Horses was but a few hours away.

He looked forward to seeing Seth Topper again, sharing a bottle of anti-fogmatic — as his old friend liked to call whiskey — while

 JASON MANNING

talking of old times. Then a hot bath at the Chinaman's watering hole, and a visit to the Regret. There was no denying that civilization had its attractions. He decided that these same amenities were why the hide hunters had not turned east, skirting the northernmost foothills of the Medicine Bow range to strike The Overland Trail where it followed the North Platte all the way down to Fort Laramie — a trip that would take three, four days if the weather was good. He assumed the hide hunters were early risers, too, and probably on the move and would reach Wild Horses before he did.

When he saw the town it was from a great distance, paused on a cut-bank where the plain began a long gradual descent to the Medicine Bow River, which was located about four hundred yards west of the town. The river was at least twice as wide as it was at the height of summer due to snow-melt. Scattered alders and cottonwoods marked its course.

There was a pall of wood smoke rising above the town and drifting towards the river. From his distant vantage point Riler couldn't tell if there were any new buildings, but the town as a whole didn't look any larger than he remembered it. Urging the buckskin forward, he set a course for the south end of Wild Horses, the wolf — which had joined him shortly after sunrise — loping alongside the horse.

As he rode into town, he passed the Regret on his left. Three women were on the long front porch, and he recognized all but one of them, the one with the willowy body and hair the color of spun gold. He remembered Ana and Molly them from his last visit, six months back. All three of them were peering up the town's one and only street, but when they became aware of his presence they smiled and waved and he touched the brim of his wide-brimmed hat as he rode on by. Up ahead, two hide-laden wagons were in front of Topper's trading post. The teamsters were still on the wagon seats, and four other men loitered on foot. He assumed they were the targets of the brothel whores' interest. Seven saddled horses and two laden with packs were hitched to the wagons.

He rode past the hide hunters, holding the buckskin to a walk, studying each one closely, just as they studied him. It was cold enough that the uncured buffalo skins weren't yet beginning to smell bad. Riler figured the men smelled worse than the hides. Some of the hunters wore deerskins, like he did, others were dressed in plain wool garb. Four of them were bearded. One of the teamsters was a burly Mexican who looked like he shaved as an afterthought. The sixth man never had to. He was full-blooded Indian, and sat on his heels on the trading post porch with his back against the wall.

The four white men were passing a bottle around. One of these, a thin, yellow-haired fellow with a lazy eye, was staring at the wolfdog and when Riler rode past he called out, "Hey mister, your dog looks like a wolf to me."

"That's 'cause he *is* a wolf, mostly" replied Riler.

"Well it better stay the hell away from me," said the hide hunter, putting his hand on the butt of an old Colt Walker that was stuck under his belt in front. The wolf looked his way then, and kept looking.

"He will," said Riler. "Unless you pull that hand cannon and aim it at him — or me."

The hide hunter tore his eyes off the wolf and met Riler's gaze and took his hand off the revolver. Riler nodded and rode on. The wolf stayed abreast of the buckskin, but looked back a few times.

The north end of town was about a hundred and fifty feet further on. On the way Riler counted buildings. Thirteen of them, all but two on the east side of the road. Those two were the Chinaman's big tent saloon, and a little further on, Gus Freeman's smithy. Wild Horses hadn't changed at all since his last visit.

The clang of blacksmith's hammer on an anvil could be heard all the way across town and as he drew near the smithy Riler saw Gus was shaping a long strip of mild steel on his anvil. A couple of new wagon wheels were propped up against one of the stout uprights that supported the roof of the long one-sided structure that shielded the forge from rain and snow. Behind the smithy was a one-room shack that Freeman called home, along with another, smaller structure used for storage. To the side was a corral, with a swaybacked sorrel mare pawing at the frost on the ground, searching for sprigs of new grass. Riler figured that the steel strips would be used as metal tires attached to the outer face of the wheels' felloes. The blacksmith was a gifted carpenter as well, and made not just wheels and other parts for wagon repairs but furniture rendered sturdy with metal brackets.

Gus Freeman was a big burly black man of about thirty years. He wore a leather apron over his broad bare chest and thick heavy gloves on his hands. Riler was acquainted with his background. Blacksmithing was a trade Gus had learned from his last owner, a man named Jessup, who had bought him from a cruel plantation owner prior to coming west at the outbreak of the War Between the States. Jessup had wanted none of that conflict, setting up a business in Santa Fe. When Jessup died a couple of years later a letter of manumission, signed and sealed, was found with his last will and testament. He gave everything to Gus, including freedom. Gus bought a wagon and some mules to pull it, loaded up all the equipment he could haul, and headed north. The war had still be raging back east and feelings running high, even in a place like Santa Fe. As far as Gus had been concerned, a town with a lot of people would include some who didn't look kindly on a former slave. He stumbled onto Wild Horses not long after it was born and settled down, taking the name Freeman because that was what he was.

Gus was humming "John Brown's Body" as he worked, but when he looked up as Riler arrived he stopped. A toothy grin flashed across his face.

"Well I'll be," he exclaimed. "Lobo Riler. You're still above snakes. Praise the Lord!" He stripped the glove off and extended his right hand as Lobo swung down off the tall buckskin and came forward to shake it.

Riler grinned and gripped Freeman's hand as tightly as he could. But it still wasn't as tight as Freeman's grip. The blacksmith had the biggest, strongest hands of anyone Riler knew, alive or dead. For a time, after being freed by his owner, Freeman had been the unrivaled arm-wrestling champion up and down both branches of the Platte River. But some people had resented being bested by a former slave, so Freeman had stopped accepting any challenges.

"How are you, Gus?" asked Riler. "And how is He'po'hehe?"

The blacksmith's face became a stoic mask, but Riler could see the pain that question caused him, a dark miasma of emotional anguish in his eyes. "My woman died this winter. Pneumonia. I took her back to her people, hopin' a medicine man might could save her. But she couldn't be saved."

Riler clamped a hand on his friend's shoulder. "I am truly sorry, Gus. Smoking Woman was a fine gal." His expression was bleak as the blacksmith's tragedy reminded him of a certain Cheyenne woman named Quahneah.

Gus nodded, looked past the mountain man and out across the plains. "I buried her out there in the grass sea. It's what she wanted. Now I know her spirit walks through the tall grass and she is happy. The Lord giveth and the Lord taketh away." His tone was forlorn.

Riler nodded. Smoking Woman had been the blacksmith's Cheyenne squaw — though Gus insisted she was his wife, not a squaw. It was a distinction Riler didn't understand, but it was the blacksmith's business how he thought of the woman he lived with and clearly loved. She had been the property of a trader named Claude Bellows, a notorious drunk and obnoxious fellow all around, who had lost his life after apparently stumbling off a cliff in a drunken state. Riler knew Gus had become enamored of the slender Cheyenne beauty while she was still warming Bellows's blankets and he had always wondered if Gus had played a role in the trader's demise. But he had never inquired and never would.

"So what about you, Lobo?" asked Gus. It was obvious he wanted to change the subject. "Still livin' all by your lonesome up in the Medicine Bow?"

"Yep. It's my home. Has been for a very long time now. Don't reckon I'll ever live anywhere else."

"I see you're still keeping that wolf."

"I don't keep him. He stays because he wants to." Riler looked over his shoulder while he spoke. The wolfdog was sitting on its haunches alongside the buckskin, its head turned, its focus on the men loitering up the street in front of the trading post. The way it sat there, jaws closed, ears pivoted in the direction it was looking, made Riler think that maybe something wasn't right at Topper's place. He went

     JASON MANNING

to the buckskin and pulled the 1852 Slant-Breech Sharps rifle out of its fringed and beaded saddle.

"I still say the 'John Brown' Spencer is a better rifle," said Gus, shaking his head. I hear tell they are making metallic cartridges for them now. You know it's named after that abolitionist who gave his men about a thousand of those rifles and then led them off to war on the slavery folk in Kansas."

Riler chuckled. "You tell me that every time I come to visit. Thanks to you I also know that some folks might call my Sharps breechloader a Beecher's Bible, on account of some preacher who said there was more moral power in one Sharps rifle than in a hundred Bibles." It didn't surprise him that Gus Freeman's idols were abolitionists. "But truth is, I'm used to this. It has never failed me." He grinned at the blacksmith. "For someone who knows a lot about guns you ought to be a better shot than you claim to be."

Gus shrugged his shoulders in a what-can-I-do gesture. "It's my eyes, Lobo. Ol' Topper give me a pair of see-betters he got in a trade some time back but they didn't do me a bit of good. No, I can't shoot worth a lick but I been told I could talk a man to death."

"I can vouch for that," he said as he untied the pack mule's lead rope from the buckskin's saddle. "Speaking of Topper, I've got some pelts here I'm of a mind to sell to him."

Gus took two long strides, reached out and grabbed Riler's arm. He let it go just as quickly, knowing how much his friend disliked being handled.

I went up there and checked on Mr. Topper a little while ago, after them hide hunters stopped at the post. They're a rough looking bunch. Look like the type who'd do just about anything if they thought they could get away with it. I asked Ol' Topper if everything was alright and, well, you know how he is. Looked plumb offended that I thought he might need some help."

Riler nodded. That sounded like Seth Topper. But he decided he would rather have Topper with his hackles up than a friend laying stone cold dead in a grave. The look of the bunch that was waiting outside the post had him a little worried about the old mountain man-turned-trader. Topper was nothing if not blunt and plain-spoken and the hide hunters struck him as men who most likely could be easily riled.

He took a step, then remembered the wolf and turned. The wolf was on its feet now, ready to accompany him. But Riler pointed at the ground and said, "You stay." The wolf sat down again, watching him intently. Riler knew it would keep watching until he was out of sight.

Chapter 4

Riler headed up the street with the Sharps in one hand and the pack mule's lead rope in the other. The hide hunters around the wagons watched him coming and when he got within earshot the man who had spoken to him earlier called out, "You got hides to sell? Well we were here first, so you'll just wait your turn."

Riler walked up to the porch and tied the lead rope to one of the uprights that supported the timbered roof. Only then did he seem to notice the man with the lazy eye. Riler's gaze was as cold as blue norther.

"I don't mind waiting my turn," he said. "What I do mind is you telling me what to do. Don't do it again."

He stood there, waiting for Lazy Eye's reaction, watching the bravado, then the doubt, and then the anger in the other man's expression. The hide hunter would either back down or fight, and Riler didn't really care which choice was made. He had an old Colt Dragoon under his belt. It wasn't that he wanted a confrontation but if he hadn't set the man straight, then the next time the two of them met it would be even more likely that there would be bloodshed.

"You have some hard bark on you, mister," said Lazy Eye resentfully. "Either that or you're plumb loco. Look around you. These are my compadres. You think they're just gonna stand around and do nothing should you start something?"

Riler smiled. He had his answer. He looked around at the other hide hunters, who were watching in grim silence, then fastened his hard, chilly gaze back on Lazy Eye.

"You mean you need them to fight your fights for you?"

"No that's not what I'm saying!"

"Then leave me alone or I'll have to fix your flint."

Riler turned for the trading post door. He could have pressed the issue, could have insisted that the man say he would no longer be a bother, but that could push Lazy Eye into doing something reckless on account of injured pride. *Then I'd have to kill him*, thought Riler. *And THEN there* would *be Hell to pay.*

He felt the eyes of all five of the hide hunters on him as he opened the door and walked into Topper's trading post. Shutting the door behind him, he looked first at the grizzled and gray-haired man behind a counter and was relieved that his old friend was unharmed. Then his gaze swept from one to the other of the five hide hunters who had turned to face him as soon as he opened the door. The sixth was on this side of the counter from Topper, and he was slow to turn around.

He was stocky, a head shorter than Riler. His leathery features were those of a man who had led a hard and dissolute life. His thick hair was black streaked with gray, his eyes dark glittering beads in a fleshy face. His jowls were stubbled. He was a mouth breather. His lips remained parted, showing yellowed teeth. Riler wondered if this was because his nose looked like it had been broken more than once and was prominently bent.

The other man planted an elbow on the countertop and leaned back, studying Riler. "And just who might you be?"

"This is Lobo Riler," said Topper. "Friend of mine, free trapper. Lobo, this here is Kelleren."

Riler's eyes narrowed. "Kelleren," he muttered.

"Well what do you know," said Kelleren. "Lobo Riler, as I live and breathe. Heard of you." He chuckled, a dry, rasping sound. "And sounds like you've heard of me."

"I have. It was nothing good."

Kelleren laughed, a loud, braying sound welling up from down deep. Riler spared the other hunters a quick look. They had been watching him warily as soon as he stepped across the threshold but now Kelleren's laughter seemed to put them at ease. A hand came off the butt of a pistol stuck in a belt, another hand dropped away from a knife sheathed to a hip.

"Well, I'll admit that most likely I should've had my toes curled long ago. It ain't for lack of people tryin' me promoted to Glory, let me tell you." He gave Riler a long look from head to toe. "Free trapper, huh? You still running traps? Still got your diggings somewhere up in the high reaches, do you?" He didn't wait for an answer. "The day of the trapper has come and gone, ol' son. Beaver ain't 'brown gold' anymore. I figured that out and moved on to hunting another critter. And this one's going to make me a rich man. I guess you saw them wagons out front so I don't need to tell you which critter I'm talking about."

"I saw the wagons."

What brings you down out of the mountains anyway?"

"I'm out of tobacco."

Again Kelleren chuckled. "My boys and me, we're out of a lot of things. Been haggling with ol' Seth here but as you know he is one on'ry cuss." He reached across the counter and clapped a meaty hand on Topper's shoulder. Then he pushed away from the counter and threw both arms out, an expansive gesture that include the five men who had come into the trading post with him. "But where are my manners? Boys, this here is Lobo Riler. A free trapper. That is to say he never signed on with no fur company. Maybe that's how he got his name. Don't reckon his pa gave it to him. It suits him right down to the ground. A lone wolf. A man who made it on his own. Something you boys couldn't do, I'll warrant." He laughed again, and clapped one of the other hunters on the shoulder. "Yessir, Lobo has been a man of the mountains for...how long now?" He looked at Riler, brows raised querulously

"Thirty years."

"And Seth Topper here, he come out with the Rocky Mountain Fur Company, so he's been in these parts more than *forty* years," Kelleren told his men. "I met Seth when I was in the beaver trade. Those were high times indeed. But they didn't last long. Times change, but some men are just too stubborn to change with 'em. Don't get much for beaver plew these days. But shaggies, that's a different story." He turned his attention to Riler. "Do you know menfolk back east ain't wearin' beaver hats these days. But they *are* wearin' buffalo coats. Yes, Sir. And the Army thinks highly of us buffalo hunters, too. Seems someone back in Washington was smart enough to figure out that a good way to do away with the Plains Injuns is to do away with the beast what gives 'em their food, their clothing, their shelter."

"That would be that bastard, Sherman," said Topper, with disdain. When the others looked at him, quizzically, he added, "The general in charge of the Army west of the Mississippi. Hand-picked by President Grant to handle the Indian 'problem.' Not surprising he is handling it like he handled the Confederacy. Not easy fighting the Plains tribes. They are more than a match for well-trained cavalry. Hard to find, hard to fight and hard to catch. So how do you whip an enemy like that? You take away his ability to make war. For the Plains Indian, that means take away the buffalo."

"What's wrong with that?" asked one of Kelleren's men, a burly, belligerent-looking fellow. Riler surmised this one had had some trouble getting through the door of the trading post.

"What's wrong with it? Same thing that was wrong about how Sherman marched through the South and let his men steal food and livestock, burn mills and crops. Women and children suffered, and some died. Broke the Confederacy's morale, disrupted its supply lines."

The big man shrugged indifferently. "So? Who cares if Injun women and children die? They're just vermin. They got no use." Then he rubbed his chin, and leered. "Well, maybe the women do...."

     Jason Manning

Kelleren grinned. "Boys, Seth here has had him some book-learnin'. Like I said, a smart feller. Smart enough to get out of the beaver business while the gettin' was good. Now he's got this post, supplyin' the locals with what they need, and both pioneers and soldiers going up the Overland Trail." Then he made a production of looking perplexed, scratching his head. "But what I don't savvy is how come he won't take the deal I made him." Glancing at Riler, he elaborated. "You see, I offered to sell him about a hunnerd buffalo skins for two dollars apiece. He can haul 'em down to the traders that camp around Fort Laramie and get three dollars for each one, easy. Now, you'd think a book-learned man would make a good businessman. And a good businessman would jump on that deal like flies on stink. Don't you think so, Lobo?"

Riler shrugged. "Maybe he doesn't have two hundred dollars."

"Uh huh, that's what he said. That he don't have that much money. But I'm not sure he's telling the gospel truth."

"Yeah, he's calling me a liar," said Topper coldly.

Riler studied his old friend's face. He could tell Topper was angry. The old trapper had a quick temper and in better days he might have taken on Kelleren and his whole gang, regardless of the odds stacked against him. On top of that, Seth didn't care for Kelleren. There was bad blood between them and had been for a long time. Riler was relieved that Topper had shown restraint — and stayed alive.

"Well, Seth," drawled Kelleren, "I know we've had our differences, you and me. But I still say a good businessman wouldn't let hard feelings get in the way of making a dollar."

"Why don't you just haul your hides down to Fort Laramie yourself?" asked Riler.

"Now that there is a good question, Lobo." Kelleren pushed away from the counter and walked over to Riler. "You see, my boys and I have this notion. West of the Medicine Bow is a herd of at least fifty thousand shaggies. No other crew is huntin' 'em out this way. We kind of think of that herd as our own."

"Yeah, a gold mine on hooves," chimed in one of the other hunters. He was a small, wiry man in buckskins, with angular features and eyes as black and cold as the Devil's. A Springfield Model 1861 long gun which had been converted into a breechloader was cradled in his arms. Riler guessed he was one of the crew's shooters.

"So we want to get back to huntin'," continued Kelleren. "Reckon we can kill twice as many if we sell our hides here instead of havin' to make the long trek to Fort Laramie. In the long run, we make more money. And then there's the bonus of gettin' to spend some time in this fine little town, with whiskey a-plenty in that Chinaman's bucket shop and some nice-smellin' quim over at the whorehouse."

"Damn right," said the big burly man.

"My balls are achin'," said another, grabbing the crotch of his woolen pants, and the others laughed — all except the one with the converted Springfield rifle, who was watching Riler.

"Well, I can't blame you boys for that," said Riler, with a twitch of his lips that some might have taken for a faint smile. "I didn't come down here just for tobacco."

Kelleren guffawed. All but the sharpshooter laughed, too. There was relief in that laughter. The hide hunters hadn't known what to expect from Riler and now they were a lot more at ease.

"But," added Riler, "looks like you're out of luck. If Seth can't — or won't — buy your hides then I reckon you'll have to come up with some other plan."

Kelleren stopped laughing. He studied Riler, then looked back at Topper. He was silent for a moment — and his men were, too.

Riler wasn't worried about Kelleren killing Topper, or even trying to beat him into taking the deal. He and Kelleren both knew the latter course of action wouldn't achieve anything.

"Maybe you're right," Kelleren said, nodding. His voice was quiet, low-pitched. His expression was inscrutable. "Guess me and my boys will go partake of the women and whiskey and give this matter some thought." He took a step towards the door then turned back to Riler. "When you've done your business here why don't you come on over to the Chinaman's and have a drink or two with me. I'm buyin'."

"Sure," said Riler.

Kelleren smiled, nodded again, and led his men out of the trading

     JASON MANNING

post. When the door closed Riler took a deep breath and let it out slowly. Topper banged a fist on the top of the counter.

"That son of a bitch," he muttered.

"That's what I've heard."

"You're right, Lobo. I don't have that kind of money. But even if I did I wouldn't do business with that bastard, not after all he's done."

"Well, you might want to consider selling those men supplies if they need any. The sooner they get out of town the better off everybody here will be. Speaking of which, where's your boy?"

Suddenly a young man stood up from behind the counter, carefully lowering the hammers on a sawed-off shotgun, which he placed on the counter. With brown eyes and skin and black hair that hung down to his shoulders and in his eyes he could have been Mexican or Indian. Riler knew him to be of Sioux-Cheyenne heritage— and Seth Topper's adopted son.

"When I saw those hide hunters coming into town I told him to get the hell out, but he would have none of it," said Topper, frowning at the boy. "I spared the rod too much, I think."

Riler smiled. "Hello, Dohasan."

Dohasan nodded gravely. "Hello, Mister Riler." He circled the counter and looked out the post's only window. Riler joined him there, while Topper was stashing the shotgun on a shelf beneath the counter. The hide hunters were in a cluster around the wagons, and then they broke up, with three men heading down the street toward the Regret, two staying with the wagons, and the other five following Kelleren as they quartered across the street in the direction of the Chinaman's.

"Looks like they're going to make themselves at home," remarked Riler.

"That's bad news," said Topper gravely. "Real bad news. If that bastard Kelleren does what he wants, nobody will be safe. This town could end up dead. And so will some of the people in it."

CHAPTER 5

Riler left the trading post window and moved to the counter, laying the Sharps long gun on top of it. He glanced round the room. It looked like a well-stocked store to him, neat and organized. A potbelly stove stood in a corner, around which were arrayed three stools. Sturdy shelves climbed two walls, laden with bags and jugs and jars and smaller metal cans. He walked over and took down one of the cans, read the label and looked at Topper. "Tomatoes?"

Topper nodded. "Canned goods, Lobo. Times, they are a-changing."

"I noticed." Riler brought the can up close to an ear and shook it, then put it back where it belonged and moved along the wall to some pouches of smoking tobacco stacked next to blocks of lard and salt. He took four of these and looked around again. On the floor were large barrels of corn, grain, beans, apples, carrots and cabbage, along with smaller casks of salted beef and large sacks of flour, rice and coffee beans. Along the side opposite the counter were a couple of sturdy tables with a stack of blankets, another stack of folded linens, baskets of buttons, ribbons and thread, some cooking utensils. Below the tables were coils of rope, lanterns, and ax handles. In the back corner was a door that Riler knew led to Topper's quarters.

"Looks like you have everything a body could possibly need or want," he said. "Got more every time I come through." He smiled at his friend. "No wonder you can't buy those buffalo hides."

"Every year there's more and more people moving up the Overland Trail, Lobo. Most of my sales are to those folks. They have come a damned long way to get here, and need some supplies before they push on over the pass. And my place is the only reliable source for those supplies between Laramie and the Divide.

Riler nodded. He figured that neither the emigrants nor the town folk had much in the way of hard money, which was why he had been pretty sure that Topper didn't have the wherewithal to buy a hundred buffalo hides at two dollars per.

"Maybe Kelleren will move on once he and his boys have had their fill of firewater and Julie Regret's girls," he remarked, as he put the smoking tobacco on the counter along with a bag each of coffee, flour and beans. "And I'll be needin' a keg of black powder along with some plugs of lead, I reckon."

Topper took a small keg from the shelf behind the counter and added it to Lobo's pile of goods.

"I'll fetch my haul," said Riler, and went outside. The two hide hunters keeping the wagons company watched him warily as he untied the pack of furs lashed to the back of his pack mule and took them inside, laying them on the counter. Topper glanced up from the bearskin that wrapped the rest of the plews and Riler smiled faintly. "Jumped me at the headwaters of Pass Creek. Got some deer, beaver and a cougar in there." He glanced at the merchandise he had brought to the counter. "I figure that and maybe five dollars will make us even?"

Topper smiled and took a metal box from under the counter, opened it, counted out three silver Liberty Dollars and one gold three-dollar piece. "More like six, I'd say. I'll hold onto your goods until you're ready to leave town." He assumed Riler would spend a day or two in Wild Horses and end up spending every last dollar before he headed home.

Riler picked up one of the pouches of tobacco. Topper reached under the counter and produced several combs of strike-anywhere matches. "Just got these lucifers in," he said. "Now you don't have to build a damn fire just to smoke your pipe."

Dohasan turned away from the window, looking to Topper. "You know this man Kelleren, father." It wasn't a question.

Riler smiled to hear the youth refer to Topper that way. Dohasan's mother had been a Sioux maiden taken by a Cheyenne brave as a war prize. When the father died in another clash with the Sioux, Dohasan and his mother had been taken in by the dead man's family. According to Topper, the mother had become an embarrassment to the family due to a habit of spreading her legs for a fair number of young bucks. Eventually she was cast out. Later, the family came to the trading post and exchanged Dohasan for a horse. Back then the trading post had been all that stood here, and the Cheyenne and Arapahos sometimes came to trade with Topper. Those days were gone, though, since animosity towards whites had soared in recent years.

Topper looked from his adopted son to Riler, and then sighed, reaching under the counter to brandish a corked jug and two metal cups. "Corn likker," he told Lobo, pulling the cork out of the jug with his teeth and filling the cups. "Made it myself. You can take the man out of Georgia, but you can't take Georgia out of the man." He picked up a cup and lifted it in a toast. "To the good ol' days."

Lobo tapped Topper's cup with his own and knocked back the moonshine. The liquid fire streaming down his gullet and exploding in his empty belly made him gasp.

Filling up the cups again, the trader glanced at Dohasan. "True, I didn't tell you about Kelleren. I wish I could forget I ever knew about him. He showed up in the mountains in 1835, the year after the Rocky Mountain Fur Company disbanded. Him and two other agents for John Jacob Astor's American Fur Company. Astor had always dreamed of monopolizing the fur trade. His agents were to recruit as many of the Rocky Mountain trappers as they could. They had some success and that's all well and good. But a good many of the men re-fused and kept trapping. Then some of those men started turning up dead or just disappeared. One of them was a good friend of mine, Luther Kane. I found his body, mutilated and scalped, the way some others had been. But from the looks of it I didn't think an Indian had taken Luther's hair. See, a Plains Indian starts to cut at the top of the forehead and around the crown and then with one hard pull the scalp pops right off. But Luther's scalp was cut off his skull. It was a messy job. The other thing is I found Luther no more than a day after he was killed and it was the dry season so it was easy enough to see that his killer rode a shod horse. Never seen an Indian's pony yet with iron on its hooves."

"But you don't know that it was Kelleren," said Dohasan.

"Not for sure, but I believe so. I followed the sign for the better part of the day. Then I lost it in some rocks and as I was trying to find it again I got shot right out of my saddle, from a distance. Bullet hit me right here." Topper touched his left shoulder below the clavicle. "There is a code among mountain men, son. One thing you don't do is bushwhack a man from hiding. If you want him dead you do it face to face. But then, Kelleren was no mountain man and he had no honor."

Topper whet his whistle with another gulp of corn liquor. "I was one of the men Kelleren tried to recruit. Told me that as far as Astor was concerned, once the Rocky Mountain Fur Company was officially disbanded every plew taken in the mountains belonged to his com-pany. Kelleren said his boss believed that free trappers were nothing more than thieves."

Dohasan thought it over, and nodded, then looked out the win-dow. "And now he's here. I don't think any of those men have honor."

"A bad man keeps bad company," said Riler.

"Their wagons are still here," remarked Dohasan.

Topper nodded. "Kelleren said he would leave 'em there since he aimed to sell the hides to me."

"But you cannot buy them," said the Indian lad. "What will they do?"

Riler and Topper exchanged glances, and the latter forced a smile when he looked at his adopted son. "Don't worry, son. Kelleren will just have to take his chances at Fort Laramie."

Riler was silent a moment, looking thoughtful, then asked, "When does the next eastbound Overland stage come through?"

"Since it's coming over the Divide that's hard to say with any certainty. It's rough going and the coaches often break down. But I would guess tomorrow or maybe the next day." Topper tilted his head, looking at Riler curiously. "Why do you ask? You don't strike me as a man who would let a stranger carry him somewhere."

"You're right about that. But I was thinking you could write a letter to whoever is in charge at Fort Laramie, find out if the Army has an interest in Kelleren. You could send Dohasan with the letter. With luck he could be back in a week or so."

Topper looked from Riler to Dohasan and back again, and then nodded. "Might not be a bad idea." To the Indian boy he said, "Go fetch me a couple of sheets of that good vellum in my desk. Pen and inkwell, too, while you're at it."

Dohasan was excited by the prospect of being given such responsibility — and he had never seen an army fort before. He hurried into the back room to do Topper's bidding.

The old trader waited until his adopted son was out of sight before saying, in a hushed tone, "Thanks, Lobo. I'm not worried about myself, but I was fretting about the boy. This will get him out of harm's way."

Riler smiled and nodded.

"However," continued Topper, "I'm thinking you know chances are good that there will be some trouble here in Wild Horses before we hear back from the fort. That or Kelleren and his crew will head on out. And I think you also know it really doesn't matter if the Army wants Kelleren or not. The bluecoats have their hands full with hostiles right now. But, regardless, thank you," he said, as Dohasan emerged from Topper's quarters with the pen, ink bottle and sheets of vellum.

     Jason Manning

"Well, I'll let you get on with your letter writing'," said Riler, and held the money he had been paid for the pelts loosely in his hand, shaking the hand so that the four coins jingled. "Reckon I'll go start spending this money. Makes me nervous being so rich."

Dohasan laughed, and Topper just smiled, already busy writing the letter that would put his son out of harm's way.

Riler left the trading post. The two men were still watching over the wagons. There were no thieves residing in Wild Horses, as far as he knew, but it was just like untrustworthy people to suspect that no one else could be trusted. The pair straightened up and watched him, as they had when he had emerged from the trading post to collect the furs he had brought, and Riler wondered what, if anything, Kelleren had told them about him.

Kelleren and the other American Fur Company agents had showed up two years before Riler had arrived in the mountains. Seth Topper had spent a couple of trapping seasons showing Riler the ropes and in that time had told the young man from Cincinnati all about his adventures in the high country. This included the story of Clete Kelleren down to every gory detail. As the years passed, and Riler got to know other free trappers he heard more stories that involved the man, all of which painted the picture of an unprincipled and dangerous individual.

Unhitching the pack mule, Riler led it back down the street towards the blacksmith forge. On the way he threw a few glances over at the big tent saloon run by the Chinaman. He heard the men talking loudly, sometimes laughing. A fiddle was screeching out a careless rendition of Stephen Foster's *De Camptown Races*. It didn't sound like anything out of the ordinary was happening inside and he continued on to Gus Freeman's smithy.

Reaching his destination, Riler found the buckskin and the wolf right where he had left them. He put the horse and mule in a corral next to the smithy so they could graze of the new grass spring grass, stripping the pack saddle off the latter and draping it over the corral's top pole. He gestured for the wolf to stay put near the corral.

Gus was on the other side of the street, at the Overland Stage

Company, talking to the station master, a man named Barstow, on the front porch. Gus earned some wages making new wheels for the Overland coaches, as well as making and applying new shoes for the teams.

With a wave at Gus, Riler headed back up the street again, the Sharps rifle cradled in his arm. This time his destination was the Regret, on the other side of town. Four of Kelleren's men had headed in that direction some time ago, and Riler wanted to spend some time with one of Julie's girls before the rest of the hide hunters made their way from the saloon to the cathouse.

As he passed the Chinaman's, Riler saw a slender man in a black suit and gold vest standing outside of the big tent, smoking a cigar. The man watched him stride past and touched the brim of his bowler. Riler had never seen him before and gave a brief but courteous nod.

The three soiled doves who had adorned the porch of the Regret when he rode into town were nowhere to be seen. He had a good idea why. No sooner had his stepped onto the porch himself than the front door opened and Julie Regret hurried out, grabbing his arm — the one the Sharps rifle wasn't draped over.

"Ever since the girls told me the man with the wolf was in town I've been looking forward to your visit, Mr. Riler."

She looked relieved, and Riler had a feeling it was more than just his money that she desired.

"Is there a problem, Mrs. Regret?"

     JASON MANNING

Chapter 6

Before she could answer there came a loud, gruff shout from inside and Julie rushed back inside, alarmed. Riler followed to see her standing at the foot of the stairs and the big burly hide hunter who earlier had opined that Indian women and children were vermin, was coming down those stairs, muttering under his breath. Julie backed up when he neared the bottom and only then did the man look up and realize she was there.

"Dammit, woman, you need more whores here!"

"Like I said when you and your friends showed up, one of you has to wait your turn," she replied, watching him warily.

"Yeah, you said. But I don't see why me and my pard couldn't share one."

Julie scowled, and put her hands on her hips, clearly perturbed. "And I told you I have a rule against that."

The hide hunter glanced at Riler, who was standing off to the side, watching intently. Then he turned his attention back to Julie and looked her over in a manner that made her uncomfortable. He stepped closer, grinning. "Then how about you and I go upstairs and every-body will be happy."

"I'm not a whore," said Julie.

"You think you're too good for me, huh? All women are whores. Now come on." He grabbed her arm.

"Let her go," said Riler.

"This is none of your business, trapper."

"I'll say it one more time. Let her go."

The hide hunter sneered. "Back off or I'll kill you."

Riler smiled faintly, nodding. "Alright then." He tilted his rifle against the wall.

The hide hunter, assuming that Riler was backing down, turned his back on the mountain man and wrenched Julie towards the stairs, his grip on her arm so tight that she cried out in pain.

Quick as lightning, Riler strode forward and laid a hand on the big hide hunter's shoulder. The man let go of Julie and whirled, throwing a roundhouse punch with his right hand, and with such force that when Riler ducked under it the hide hunter lost his balance and pitched forward. Riler balled up a fist and slammed it with all his might into the other's gut. It was like hitting a tree trunk. The hide hunter was big, but he was quick. He brought his right arm round the other way and this time his fist connected with Riler's head in a backhand blow that knocked the mountain man off his feet. He hit the floor hard and slid a few feet.

"I'm gonna kill you and skin you and I ain't decided which I'll do first," snarled the hide hunter as he drew a long blade from the sheath on his hip.

Riler got to his feet. As he backed up he considered the Navy Re-volver stuck in his belt. But he pulled his knife instead. He didn't want to kill this man if he could help it, and when guns came into play death was the end result, more often than not. Besides that, a sense of fair play managed to intrude into his thinking. The hide hunter had drawn a knife, so he was obliged to do the same.

The hide hunter chuckled. "What's wrong? You scared? You can't get away from me!"

 JASON MANNING

Still backing up, Riler found himself in the Regret's well-furnished parlor. He could see Julie behind the hide hunter. She was rubbing her arm, all the color drained from her face. He was about to call to her to run when she spun around and fled into the dining room, turning left in the direction of the kitchen. With the woman out of harm's way he lunged at the hide hunter, who braced himself and pulled his right arm back, ready to plunge his knife into Riler when he arrived.

But Riler didn't arrive the way the other man expected. As the hide hunter's right arm began to come forward, Riler dropped into a forward roll on his left shoulder, and once his back was flat on the floor he bent his knees and kicked out. His left foot collided with the hide hunter's knife arm, propelling it into his body. The right foot slammed into his adversary's left leg above the knee with such force that it might have broken the leg of an ordinary man. But the hide hunter was no ordinary man. His leg didn't snap but it buckled. As he went down, Riler was rolling over and getting to his feet.

The big man was quick to rise, too, but he was unsteady on the hurting leg, growling like a wild animal and trying to keep Riler at bay by swinging his knife wildly back and forth in front of him. Riler stepped into a swing, throwing his shoulder into the other man's chest to keep him off balance, and slashing at the back of the hide hunter's knife hand, cutting tendons. The man howled and the knife slipped from useless fingers. Riler then kept pivoting his body until his back was against the other, and brought his left arm up, bent, driving his elbow into the his adversary's face and hearing the satisfying crack of cartilage.

His nose broken, the hide hunter staggered blindly. Riler stepped back, switched the knife to his left hand, drew the Navy Revolver from his belt, flipped it so that he was holding it by the barrel and used the butt to club the other man senseless. The floor shook under his feet when the unconscious hide hunter fell. Only then did Riler see Julie, crossing the hallway, lowering a meat cleaver she had held raised up high. She looked down at the unconscious man and then at Riler and said, "You should have shot him dead."

Riler just shook his head and stepped into the hall, putting himself between Julie and another hide hunter, this one a tall, wiry fellow with a pock-marked face, coming down the stairs in a hurry, a pistol in hand. When he realized he was looking down the barrel of the mountain man's Navy Revolver he froze. Riler watched the man's eyes move to his friend sprawled on the parlor floor, saw his hand tighten on the butt of his pistol, saw it start to come up.

"Don't," snapped Riler, "or I'll kill you where you stand."

The second hide hunter slowly lowered the pistol, glaring at the mountain man. "If Breck is dead, so are you," he muttered.

"He isn't dead." Riler backed up, in the process herding Julie through the doorway into the dining room. "Go ahead," he told the other man. "See for yourself."

The hide hunter gave a curt nod and eased on down the stairs, then crossed the hall and knelt beside the one called Breck. He saw that his friend was breathing, then studied Breck's bleeding hand, and looked up at Riler bleakly.

"That hand ain't ever gonna be right again," he said. "Maybe you should've kilt him, 'cause when he comes to he'll be wantin' to skin you alive."

"Yeah," said Riler. "He said that before, and look what happened to him. Now unless you can carry him all by yourself go fetch your friends and take him out of here."

The pock-marked man rose. "I don't take orders from you. I only take orders from Kelleren."

"Sure. Consider it advice, then. But just do it."

The man looked down the barrel of the Navy Revolver, held steady and true — and stuck his own pistol into his waistband. "They ain't done doing what they come here to do," he muttered, but he went on up the stairs.

"You're bleeding on my floor, Mr. Riler," said Julie quietly.

"What?" Riler looked down at the floor and saw the drops of blood, then at his left hand and the blood channeling down his long fingers and finally at the three-inch tear high on the sleeve of his deerskin shirt. Breck had gotten him with one of his wild swings, but he hadn't felt anything — until now. He winced when he moved his arm,

     JASON MANNING

bending it at the elbow, to hold the hand against his chest to prevent more blood from dripping on the floor.

"Come to the kitchen, I'll tend to it."

Riler shook his head and looked up the stairs. He could hear male voices, angry and argumentative. "Not yet." A moment later the three hide hunters came single-file down the staircase, two of them still in the process of dressing. They glowered belligerently at Riler but no one said anything to him. He kept the Navy Revolver in hand until they carried the unconscious Breck out the front door.

Crossing the threshold, one of them looked at Julie and said, "We'll be back."

Julie nodded, her expression inscrutable, and she closed the door behind the hide hunters and returned to Riler as he shoved the pistol under his belt. "Now, to the kitchen. Let me take a look at your arm." Ana showed up right then at the top of the stairs, buttoning the top button of her camise. "Ana, there's blood here on the floor, and in the parlor, too."

"*Si, Señora,*" said Ana.

Julie took Riler by the good arm, knowing she didn't need to tell Ana what to do about the mess, and took him through the dining room into the kitchen, where she sat him in one of the chairs at the small table. She put down the cleaver and poured some well water into a pot and put the pot on top of the stove. Then she opened up a small trunk and pulled out a frayed length of linen which she tore into long strips. Riler noticed her hands were shaking a bit.

Ana came in to fetch a bowl of warm water and a rag, smiled at Riler and went out again without a word. Then came a knock on the door and Riler's hand closed around the butt of his pistol as he rose from the chair.

"You sit down," said Julie sternly. "I'll get it."

"No. You stand back a ways."

Riler threw the door open and lowered the pistol when he saw Dohasan standing there. The Indian lad looked at the Navy Revolver, then up at Riler.

"Father sent me to make sure you were well," he explained.

Julie had a bowl of hot water in hands protected by clean towels as she peered past the mountain man and said, "He'll be fine. Run along now and tell Seth as much. I need to tend to Mr. Riler's wounds."

Dohasan nodded and loped off. Riler closed the door, put the pistol on the table and eased himself down into a chair. He managed to peel the shirt off over his head, wincing as he had to lift the wounded arm, while Julie pulled the other chair around the table so she could sit in front of her patient, glancing at the scars on the mountain man's chest and belly, wondering how many of those old wounds had been self-treated. Probably all of them, she decided, if they had been treated at all.

"I have some laudanum," she said, glancing up into his intense blue gaze. Riler just shook his head. She dabbed at the blood oozing out of the cut. "It's deep but not too deep." she decided, basing that initial diagnosis on the amount of blood. Dipping the cloth into the bowl and wringing it out, she began to gently clean the wound. "Get it cleaned a bit and then I'll sew it up and dress it."

"I can close it up."

Julie glanced at his old scars again. "I know you can, but it doesn't hurt quite as much when someone else does it." She smiled, and he answered with a grim smile of his own. "Besides, I think I'm probably better at it than you are. I've had a fair amount of practice mending folks. My man, Moke…" She shook her head with a soft, pensive laugh. "He was a careless and sometimes very clumsy man." A shadow of melancholy fell across her visage and extinguished her smile.

Riler's head swiveled as he looked towards the door to the dining room. He had heard footsteps, soft ones, but he was wary nonetheless. It was the golden-haired whore, Rose. She looked disheveled. Her camise was open, revealing her pert young breasts. As it had been nearly a year since he had last laid eyes on a woman's breasts, Riler stared unashamedly. Noticing this, Rose flashed a saucy little smile.

"Well now I know why those fellas lit out," she said. "It's the man with the wolf."

"Lobo Riler is his name, Rose," said Julie, as she stood to go to the trunk again. "You wouldn't remember him. He was here before the first snow last year, maybe a month before you showed up at my door."

"Better late than never!" said Rose, eyes bright. "It's a pleasure to make your acquaintance, Mr. Riler?"

"Maybe." His eyes continued to boldly roam.

Rose grinned.

"Lace up, Rose," said Julie, as she returned to the table with a needle and thread.

"Yes, Miss Julie. I'm kind of glad those smelly hide hunters are gone. The one with me said he wasn't finished yet, and would come back to do so. I told him it would cost him another dollar. He wasn't happy. But those are the rules. Right, Miss Julie?"

"That's right." Julie sat down and began threading the needle. "Now you might want to go clean up. I reckon there'll be more of those hide hunters showing up today. Besides, you're squeamish and you won't want to watch this."

Once Rose was gone and the needle was threaded, Julie looked at Riler. "You ready?"

"As I'll ever be," he replied. He focused on her face as she leaned in and pushed the needle into the swollen, angry flesh round the gash. He clenched his teeth, his body stiffened, but his gaze was unwavering.

That made Julie self-conscious, so she began to talk. "I'm awfully glad you came when you did, Mr. Riler. I shudder to think what would have happened if you hadn't been here. I just pray it won't lead to more trouble for you."

"Life's full of trouble."

She glanced at him again, and could sense that he was made uncomfortable by her gratitude, so she fell silent. She finished stitching up the wound, cleaned it with iodine, and dressed it with two of the strips of linen. When she was done Riler thanked her and put one of the Liberty dollars on the table.

"What's that for?" she asked, thinking he intended to pay her for tending to his wound — a payment she was not going to accept.

"The yellow-haired girl," said Riler, with a smile, and reached for his deerskin shirt.

She grabbed it first. "Well you may as well let me clean and sew that up to while you're upstairs," she said flatly.

He nodded and left the kitchen. When his back was turned she looked at him, and when she heard his footsteps on the staircase, she sighed — then silently scolded herself for thinking of a man other than her husband in that particular way.

CHAPTER 7

When they were done, Riler and Rose lay tangled up in the sheets, he on his back and she with her slender body molded against his side. He had his fingers tangled in her mussed golden hair and she had her head on his right shoulder, eyes closed. She had told him that he had "worn her out" and that she needed to rest a bit and would he hold her while she did. Riler tried not to make more of that request than was warranted, reminding himself that she had previously entertained one of the hide hunters and that this, not his prowess in bed, was the cause of her exhaustion.

Still, he lay there quietly, though he acknowledged the danger in doing so, because the sensation of having a naked woman molding her body to his in the aftermath of passion produced vivid memories of Quahneah. Rose lay there, a leg thrown over his, her head on his chest, her arm draped across his chest, and he could tell by her breathing that she had drifted off to sleep. Despite the fact that she was a whore there was a tenderness to the way she clung to him that was endearing.

Contact with others brought him back to life, to some extent, after his Indian wife's passing. These past few years he had made use of the other Regret whores, Molly and Ana, but neither of them had asked to be held, or shown any inclination to lay with him after the deed was done. It had been physical release for him and strictly business for them.

In retrospect, he was glad of that, even though at the time he had been a little put off by their lack of passion. Now that he was with Rose he realized how dangerous it was to linger in a woman's arms. He missed the intimacy and that made him miss Quahneah all the more. After her death he had reconciled himself to living the rest of his life alone. It was not something he had vowed to do. He had simply assumed this was his fate and he accepted it.

But now, laying with Rose, he began to wonder if he *had* to live alone. He was struck by the contrast of his hand, scarred and big-knuckled and browned by long exposure to the elements, resting on the pale, warm, satin-smooth curve of the blonde girl's hip. And she *was* a girl to him, a young and beautiful woman-child, the kind that could engender not just raging lust in a man but the desire to protect.

It would be nice to have a woman's company again, Riler thought. A woman he could think of as his own. But just entertaining such a thought produced a fresh wave of guilt. Many times he had told Quahneah that she was his life and he had meant it. And even dead she was still his life. That, he told himself, was the way it *should* be. Even if it meant living a life that sometimes hardly seemed worth living anymore.

"Damn it," he muttered, angry at himself, He moved, slowly extricating his arm from under Rose, hoping not to disturb her rest. He sat on the edge of the bed, head down, running fingers through his thick tousled hair, pushing it back and out of his face. This caused a twinge of pain in his wounded arm. There was inherent risk in contact with other people. The risk of becoming involved in one way or another. And becoming involved meant the risk of caring. Why had he gotten involved when the hide hunter had threatened to drag Julie Regret upstairs and have his way with her? It was none of his business. But the answer was obvious. Because what the hide hunter wanted to do was wrong — and to stand by and let it happen would have been even more wrong. And now, quite possibly, he had Kelleren and the whole crew of hide hunters to deal with.

Riler rose and went to the room's single window. Since the room was at the back of the house all he could see were golden-brown plains and distant snow-clad mountains to the east, mountains that had been named after the Laramie River, which in turn had been named after a French-Canadian trapper who had disappeared in those mountains about fifty years ago. Giving in to a growing melancholy, he was thinking he ought to get back to the Medicine Bow Mountains and disappear, too — but then Rose stirred and saw him standing there and slipped out of bed and came up behind him without bothering with clothes, wrapping her arms around his midsection and laying her cheek against his back.

"You're nice and warm," she murmured.

"It's cold in here," he allowed.

Her hand began to roam slowly down across his taut belly, and she arched her back to press her pert young breasts against him. Riler reached down and placed his hand over hers and stopped it.

"I should be going," he said. "No offense."

"If it's about money, you don't need to worry. I like being with you."

She sounded so sincere, and Riler wondered why his first thought was that she more than likely had said that very same thing to other customers. He turned and held her gently at arm's length, hands on her shoulders, and gave into weakness, gazing at her lissome, naked body. Then an image from the past ambushed him — of Quahneah climbing into their bed wearing a sultry smile and nothing else. He let go of Rose and stepped around her, moving to the ladderback chair where his clothes, boots, possibles bag and weapons had been stashed. "I better get going," he said gruffly.

"Whatever you say," she said, disappointed, and turned to untangle a quilt from the sheet and draped the former around her shoulders and plopped down on the edge of the sagging mattress and started to sulk, while Riler pulled on his buckskin breeches. He thought he had hurt her feelings and it occurred to him that maybe even whores needed a moment of intimacy. With that in mind, he forgot about his clothes, walked over to sit beside her and put an arm round her.

"Truth is," he said, "I'd rather be here."

She looked at him earnestly. He sounded genuine — it sounded almost like a confession — but she was cautious in her own right. "Really?" she asked. "You mean that?"

"Yes, ma'am."

Rose poked him in his good arm, playfully. "Don't call me that. You're old enough to be my pa."

"Ouch," said Riler, feigning a wince.

She laid a hand on his muscle-corded thigh and laughed softly. "But no one has ever done me the way you just did me. I mean, no one has ever made me feel…" She stopped, seeking the right words, looking flustered.

Riler studied her with a healthy dose of skepticism — until she looked away from him and he noticed she was clearly blushing and there was something about her reaction that slipped past his defenses and touched his heart.

"I better go," he said gruffly and stood up.

"Wait," she whispered, and went after him, threw her arms round him again. Riler chided himself for his cynicism. Because in that single word Rose had uttered he heard an emotion he was all too familiar with — loneliness. He turned round in her arms for a second time and as she clung to him tightly he felt a fierce desire rise up in him, as it had when he had first lain down with Rose an hour ago.

Riler had a strong will. He could deny himself food and rest and shelter, when the situation called for sacrifice. But he could not resist slipping his brawny arms under the quilt and around Rose in that moment, pulling her to him. She let go of the quilt and it fell to the floor around her feet and as soon as he felt her slender, naked, eager body against him, he knew he had to have her again.

"No one has ever made you feel what?" he asked.

Rose looked surprised as she touched one of her reddening cheeks. She couldn't remember the last time she had actually blushed. "Other

     JASON MANNING

men who visit me, they say all kinds of things. How pretty I am. How they've fallen in love with me. How this and how that I am. But what they really only care about is this." She put a hand on her belly and let it slide downward until her fingertips touched the soft golden forest of her untrimmed pubic hair. At the same time her other hand left her very rosy cheeks and came to rest on his chest, and those fingers played in his chest hair. "But you," she murmured, looking up at him with big, earnest blue eyes, "...you make me feel like you want all of me." She frowned and shook her head. "No, that's not the right word. You *need* all of me. Or am I imagining things?"

Riler was solemn and silent for a moment, dwelling on just how powerful an emotion loneliness was, realizing then that perhaps all along he had come to the Regret not just for sexual release but also to experience the psychological pleasure of a woman's company, the sensation of her body against his, a breath, a scent, a smile. He imagined having Rose Waldron with him up in the high country, sharing his cabin with her, waking up to her every morning, and there was much about such mental images that was appealing.

But then he thought about Quahneah. While she could be soft and needful and sensual, Quahneah had been Cheyenne above all else and perfectly capable of fending for herself. She had been as deadly with her bow and arrows as he was with the Sharps. He had always been confident she would be just fine when he rode off to trap or hunt or just look for any sign that 'his' mountain had been intruded upon by strangers. He had to wonder if this soft, pale, delicate woman-child in his arms could do the same, if she could endure the hardships he took for granted.

"Well," he said, slowly, struggling to find the right words. "No, you're not imagining things but..."

And then she had her arms locked around his neck, and a flurry of hot wet kisses cut him off, and for once Riler was not willing to go without. His arms tightened around her slender waist and he stepped forward and they fell onto the bed and her legs locked round his midsection and he hurriedly fumbled with his breeches and then she was moaning softly in that moment of joining when the rest of the world simply disappeared.

This time it was not as frenzied as the first, more lovemaking than pure lust, and for that reason Riler thought about Quahneah at the most inopportune moment. But he continued until Rose had reached her peak, and then he disengaged from her clinging arms and legs and looked down at her with a troubled brow. Rose propped herself up on her elbows and looked back at him, her contented smile fading as she studied his face.

"What's wrong?" she asked in a soft, worried voice.

Riler wondered how he could express the guilt that had suddenly overcome him and gave up with a shake of his head. He began to dress quickly.

It was Rose's turn to be at a loss for words. She sat up on the edge of the bed with shoulders bunched and hands clasped between her knees, looking out the window in a way that made Riler think she wasn't admiring the scenery or even seeing it. He knew what was wrong and, worse, knew he had hurt her. He had foolishly entertained the notion that he didn't have to be alone any more, and in the process had given her hope that she didn't have to be, either. And now he was backing out on her. Once dressed, he stepped over to the bed and put a hand on her bare shoulder.

"Rose…"

She shrugged his hand away. Riler began digging into the coin pouch tied to his belt and she said, flatly, "Give Miss Julie the dollar."

Grabbing his rifle, Riler fled the room. Going down the stairs, he heard someone in the kitchen and headed that way. Julie was stirring the contents of a large blackened cast-iron pit atop the stove. The aroma of the pot's contents mingled with the smell of the fire burning in the stove's belly should have made his belly knot. He hadn't eaten anything since partaking of some jerked venison in camp the night before. But he had lost his appetite.

When he entered she glanced at him briefly, then turned her attention back to the pot. "You can leave the dollar on the table," she said.

Riler nodded and did so. "Thanks for sewing me up."

She nodded. "Stew's about ready if you want some. On the house."

She didn't look at him.

"Thanks, but I better get going." He sensed that she was uncomfortable in his presence — or maybe it was just indifference — and that she was just being polite in offering a meal. Mystified, he shook his head and left the kitchen.

Emerging from the Regret he nearly ran into the man in the black suit and gold vest he had seen loitering in front of the Chinaman's tent saloon earlier.

"You must be the one those men in the saloon are talking about," said the man.

"Could be," said Riler.

"The name's Caulfield. Eldon Caulfield. And you are?"

"Riler."

"Pleased to make your acquaintance, Mr. Riler. Are you a hide hunter, too?"

"Nope."

"I'm an army officer, retired. And formerly a lawman."

Caulfield waited, expecting Riler to ask at least one of the questions other people generally asked him when he spoke of his past vocations, such as which side he had fought for in the war, or the name of the town where had he worn a tin star. But Riler just nodded and didn't seem at all interested in his history.

"Well, apparently some of those buffalo hunters would like to see you dead. It seems you did considerable damage to one of their number. I just came over to make sure everyone was alright," said Caulfield.

"The womenfolk are fine," Riler assured him, then glanced past him and saw Kelleren emerge from the tent saloon and begin to quarter across the street towards the cathouse. He was alone.

Caulfield followed Riler's gaze and looked over his shoulder. "Here comes trouble," he murmured.

"Why don't you go inside and check on the women yourself. I reckon he's coming to parlay with me."

"I'll stand with you, sir." Caulfield laid a hand on the pistol in his belt.

"No you won't," snapped Riler. He didn't cotton to the idea of getting killed thanks to someone who had something to prove — and Caulfield struck him as one of those. "Either move off this porch or go inside."

Caulfield looked at the mountain man, startled. "I assure you, Sir…."

Riler's cold blue eyes narrowed as he fastened them on the other man. He didn't fight alongside a fellow he didn't know. A stranger could turn out to be a hindrance rather than an asset. Caulfield might have been a war veteran and a fearless lawman — or he might be a liar. Not that he expected Kelleren to fight. Had that been the man's intent he would have brought the other hide hunters along. But even if Kelleren just wanted to talk — or threaten — Riler didn't cotton to the idea of a stranger sticking a nose in what he considered his personal business.

Offended, Caulfield turned and entered the Regret without another word.

A moment later Kelleren arrived at the foot of the porch steps and squinted up at Riler, eyes narrowed against the bright midday sunlight. The mountain man had leaned his good shoulder against an upright and was packing tobacco into the bowl of his pipe, the Sharps cradled in his arm. Kelleren tilted his head and folded his arms, chuckling.

"You look almighty calm for feller who has about a half-dozen men wantin' to kill you."

Riler finished packing the bowl and clenched the stem of the pipe between his teeth. He broke a strike-anywhere off one of the combs Topper had given him, struck it on the upright and held the flame to the pipe bowl, puffing a few times until the tobacco was burning nicely.

"Well to be honest," drawled Kelleren, "Only about a few of 'em want you dead. The rest are talking about breaking your arms or legs or takin' your hair and leavin' you alive to suffer."

"And where do you come down?"

"To tell you the truth, at first I was on the side of killing you stone dead. Back in that trading post I got the feeling you were nothing but trouble. But since then I've been thinking you're a man who is willing to live and let live. I mean, after all, you could've killed Breck but you didn't. Though, knowing him as I do, I expect sooner or later you may have to."

Riler was silent as the other man climbed the steps and leaned against another upright. He understood that a man like Kelleren didn't fancy looking up to anyone.

"I finally got what I believe to be the gospel truth from those boys what were in this cathouse when you crippled Breck," drawled Kelleren. "It was plumb wrong what he tried to do with the madam of this fine establishment. The fact that you bought a whole world of trouble by not killing him makes me think you don't *want* trouble. Also tells me you're a right smart man, even if you don't look it. Had you taken his life you would have had to lose yours and no telling who else would have, too. You know how men like mine can get when their dander is up."

Riler smoked and nodded.

Kelleren pushed off the upright and took two steps forward, so that he was face to face with the mountain man. "Here's my proposition, Mr. Riler, so listen well. My men will leave you alone, and in return you will leave them alone. They'll leave that madam and every other living soul in this town alone, too. Except for the whores."

Riler thought it over, grimly chiding himself for not at all liking the idea of one of the hide hunters laying with Rose. "Sounds alright."

"Ha!" grunted Kelleren, grinning as he shuffled a gleeful little dance step. "God damn! I knew you were a reasonable man! There's just one more thing. When I go back to your friend Topper to try to work out a deal with him about those buffalo hides, you'll have already talked into him to take my offer."

"I could try to persuade him all day long but that won't produce two hundred dollars for him to pay you for those hides."

"Well now, don't you worry about that. Maybe he won't have to. I'm a reasonable man, too, you see. So, do we have a deal, Mr. Riler?"

Riler looked past Kelleren, down the street of Wild Horses, thinking about Gus and Seth and Julie and her girls and the other residents, knowing that in all likelihood a lot of them — maybe all of them — might die if he declined the deal and did what he wanted to do, which was to kill this man right here and now. Not in self-defense, but in a reckoning for the free trappers Kelleren and his American Fur Company cohorts had killed thirty years ago — and also because he was in a foul mood. If he didn't go along, Kelleren would let loose his dogs of war. Riler had no illusions about how that would end. He would die. He might be able to take some with him, but the odds were too steep. Even worse, Seth and Gus would probably feel compelled to get involved, and they would die, too.

He nodded. "We do."

Kelleren flashed his yellowed teeth in a big grin. "Good, good! Let's drink on it." He turned and headed for the Chinaman's tent saloon.

Riler hesitated, wondering if everything Kelleren had said before was part of a ruse to get him into the tent saloon — and right into an ambush. Then he realized how unlikely that was. Had Kelleren wanted him dead he would have come to the Regret with all his men, and that would have been that.

Pipe clenched in his teeth, Sharps rifle cradled in his arm, buffeted by a cold wind sweeping down off the snowy high reaches, Riler followed the hide hunter chief across the wide, rutted street.

Chapter 8

When he came up to the tent saloon, Riler noticed that a small plank sign was hanging from the thick cedar post, the first of a row of fifteen-foot-tall posts along the centerline of the saloon which held up the peak of the large and weather-worn canvas roof of the establishment. The words 'the Celestial' were carved on the plank. He assumed that this was the name that Long Woo — otherwise known hereabouts as the Chinaman — had given his business.

Stepping past the post and into the shade of the huge tent, Riler's icy blue eyes swept the interior, which was about forty feet long and thirty wide, open at the rear just as it was in front. Its northern and southern sides consisted of log walls the height of an average man, to which the sides of the tent were secured. There was no floor, just hard-pack dirt. There were a couple of stone-ringed fire pits in the middle, each between two center poles. The crackling fires in the pits kept the place fairly warm. To Riler's right was a long counter, boards placed atop barrels. Behind this were a row of what looked like four coffins laid end to end on the ground, but were actually homemade chests in which Woo kept the liquor he sold under lock and key. To the left were square tables encircled by stools with an occasional chair thrown into the mix.

The only people sitting at those tables were Kelleren and his hide hunting crew — or seven of them anyway. Riler saw no sign of Breck, and by his count there was another one missing, the Indian he had seen sitting on his haunches in front of the trading post that morning. By the sound of things, some of them were well on their way to drunkenness. The volume of their loud and boisterous chatter dropped considerably when Riler stepped inside, and some of them glared at the mountain man. He made eye contact with every one of them and then turned towards the bar, presided over by Long Woo and one of his sons.

Riler laid the Sharps atop the bar and fished a Liberty dollar out of his possibles pouch, which he handed to Woo. The mountain man knew that Woo often watered down the whiskey he bought from Laramie and had transported via the Overland Trail, and he didn't blame the man for doing so, considering the expense incurred in acquiring the rotgut. Woo also bought some of Seth Topper's homemade moonshine, but that was always in limited supply and therefore expensive.

"Whiskey," said Riler, and added, "the good stuff."

Woo looked at him inscrutably, giving no indication he remembered Riler from previous visits, or their first meeting, during which the mountain man had fiercely complained about being served watered-down red-eye by one of the Chinaman's sons. Woo nodded and turned to unlock one of the trunks, producing a full, unmarked bottle of amber liquid which he placed before Riler along with an enamel cup. Riler uncorked the bottle, filled the cup nearly to the top, and took an exploratory sip, then nodded his approval and gulped down the cup's contents.

"That's the genuine article," he gasped as he refilled his cup.

"Riler!" This was Kelleren, calling from his table. "Come on over and let me introduce you proper-like to the ruffians and no-accounts what follow me!"

        JASON MANNING

Riler glanced over his shoulder. "In a minute," he said, then turned back to Woo. "You still have baths out back?"

Woo nodded, but he was looking past Riler at the hide hunters. He leaned forward and spoke with his voice pitched low. "You think your friends pay for all they drink?"

Again Riler looked over his shoulder, and this time counted five bottles either sitting on the three tables occupied by Kelleren's crew or held in hand. Turning back to Woo he shrugged.

"I couldn't say. They aren't friends of mine. As I recall you always required payment before a drink is poured."

Woo was a tall, slender man with a mustache that dangled below his jawline. Topper had told Riler that Woo had shown up in a gold town on the American River some twelve years ago with his young wife. They had fled the violence of the Taiping Rebellion in China. Woo and his bride had done the laundry of the prospectors and miners for free. No one cared enough about them to wonder how they could survive without making any money. But when Woo left the gold fields behind him he was well-off by frontier standards, having collected hundreds of dollars' worth of gold dust from the clothing he had washed. He had also learned how to speak English and parlayed that skill into getting a job as a recruiter of Chinese laborers for the Central Pacific Railroad. Why he had shown up in Wild Horses a few years ago, where he wasn't likely to make much if any profit at all from his saloon, he didn't say. Topper surmised he had gotten into trouble with the law, or with one of the tongs that had arisen in San Francisco's Chinatown, and had found in Wild Horses an out-of-the-way place to disappear.

"It is my custom," admitted Woo gravely. "But their leader, the gray-haired one, said he was good for it and to not take his word would be an insult. I am not afraid for my own life." He glanced out the back of the tent saloon, where two smaller tents were located, one where his wife and three children did laundry, the other containing the bath. "But I fear for my family."

Riler nodded. "You're right to do so." He plugged the bottle with the cork, leaving the cup, and fetched the Sharps as he turned towards the tables.

The hide hunters fell silent as he approached. Kelleren leaned forward and spoke to a man at his table and the man grabbed a bottle and vacated his chair, moving to another table. Kelleren kicked the empty chair out a bit as Riler arrived. Riler turned it around so that it was backed up to the table. That way he could rise and step back without having to deal with the chair getting in the way. He laid the Sharps across his lap so that no one could knock it down if he tilted it against the table, or even reach for it quicker than he could lay hands on it.

"Good of you to join us, Lobo," said Kelleren. "I was telling the boys about some of the mountain men I met or knew about, like Beckwourth, who became a Crow war chief, and Bridger, who explored the high country from the geysers along the Yellowstone to the salt lake down Utah way. About how folks call John. C. Fremont 'The Pathfinder' but it was a mountain man named Kit Carson, not Fremont, who led the expedition through California and Oregon."

Riler nodded. "You know your history. Good men, all. But I'm not in their league. I don't have a pass or a fort or a river named after me. I never signed on with a fur company. I've always been a free trapper."

"Hell, I didn't know there were any of your kind left up in the mountains," said one of the other men at the table.

"Used to be hundreds," said Kelleren. "Now...." He shrugged, and looked at Riler. "How many of your kind would you say are left up in the high country?"

Riler shrugged. "Don't know. Not many." He uncorked the bottle and took a swig.

"Well, it don't matter. One thing is certain. Not a damned thing lasts forever. Since we're all going to get along while we're here I want to introduce you to my men." He gestured at the other two men at the table. They were young fellows who bore a striking resemblance to one another, lanky and tall, with shaggy brown hair and muddy-brown eyes in round faces. One of them wore a battered Confederate forage cap. "These are the Heller boys, Billy and Emmett. Billy is one of my shooters, a crack shot with long gun or short. Emmett is our cook. He's a damn fine belly cheater, too. Make someone a fine wife

        JASON MANNING

was he inclined in that direction." Kelleren chuckled, as did some of the others. As you can see, they're twins. They and three other brothers fought for the South in the late, great war. They're the only ones who survived. They went home to Louisiana after Lee surrendered but before long they came out here and signed on with me."

"It was bad enough that the damned Union was givin' all them slaves they freed forty acres and a mule," muttered one of the Heller brothers sullenly. "But my Pa had a tobacco farm and the damned carpetbaggers who ran the Reconstruction government in Louisiana made it so he couldn't find enough workers, since they were payin' the damned nigrahs to work the fields the Yankees confiscated. So then he couldn't pay the land tax and he lost the place."

"Next day he went out into the swamp," said the other Heller. "Said he was goin' hunting. Never saw him again. Our ma and sister went to New Orleans lookin' for work, and ended up whorin'. Weren't nothin' left for us back there."

Riler nodded — and wondered if the Heller boys knew there was a freed slave in Wild Horses. He hoped not, for Gus Freeman's sake.

Kelleren gestured at the four men sitting around a nearby table. "That feller in the buckskins, that be Jim Early." Riler glanced at the small, wiry man who had been watching him like a vulture in Topper's trading post earlier in the day. His Springfield rifle was leaning against the table within easy reach. "All he'll say about his past is that he's was a scout for the Army. Been in a good many scrapes with Injuns. And I can vouch for the fact that he is one hell of a marksman. The one to Jim's left, I think you know him from the local whorehouse."

Riler nodded again. It was the man who had confronted after he had beaten Breck.

"That's Texas Jack. He's my wrangler, looks after the mules and horses. Was a cowboy who helped push cattle up the Chisholm Trail for a couple years until he got into some kind of trouble. He won't say what kind, exactly, so my guess is he's got paper out on him." Kelleren grinned crookedly and leaned over to pretend he was saying something confidentially to Riler, but said it loud enough for all present to hear. "I suppose he's afraid we might decide to collect the bounty. But Jack there fancies the ladies but I don't reckon they fancy him that much."

This elicited chuckles from some of the other hide hunters. Texas Jack took a swig from a bottle, wiped his mouth on his sleeve and shrugged. "Who gives a good goddamn what a whore fancies?"

"That codger next to Texas Jack is named Mac McNally." Riler took this man to be at least fifty winters old, with an unkempt, tobacco-stained beard, and narrowed slits for eyes beneath shaggy brows. His skin was brown and looked like old whang-leather. He was carving something into the top of the table with an Arkansas Toothpick. Riler had already noticed that there were a couple more knives sheathed to his belt. "Him and Breck, the man you quarreled with at the Regret, are our skinners. Known him the longest of any of 'em. He and I worked for the American Fur Company together. He's not much for talkin' or drinkin' or whorin' but he sure knows his way around blades. He could skin you in nothing flat, Lobo."

Mac turned his head and spat a stream of tobacco juice onto the hardpack, then fastened his squint on Riler. "Sure I could. Or I could keep you alive all day and just skin ya a little piece at a time."

The other hide hunters looked from the skinner to Riler, wondering if the mountain man might take offense at such a comment.

"Well," said Riler, "I reckon everybody has to be good at something."

Kelleren's laugh boomed like thunder rolling through the tent saloon. The others relaxed.

Riler looked at the fourth man seated at the nearby table. This was the one who had confronted him on the porch of Topper's trading post, the one with the lazy eye, whom Kelleren introduced as Jonah Johnson. Johnson was studiously ignoring Riler, focused instead on polishing off the contents of a nearly-empty bottle of rotgut.

"JJ is one of my reloaders. The other one is that red savage sittin' at the next table, with the darkie." Kelleren chuckled. "That Injun is called Chaytan. Means 'hawk' in the lingo of the Dakota Sioux. He understands the King's English but he can't speak. Seems someone cut out his tongue. Probably insulted a war chief. But we'll never know for sure — since he can't tell us!" Kelleren guffawed and again some

     JASON MANNING

of the others chuckled. "As for the nigrah, that's Morris. Now he's one man who'd have to pay rent at the Regret were we going to stay in this one-horse town for long. He has this thing for white women. He looked at one a little too long some twenty years back over in Charleston and was whipped near to death. There couldn't have been much meat left on his back because it's an unholy mess to this day. But some people never learn their lesson. And the women don't mind the scars."

"'Cause his spicket is so damn big," said Jonah Johnson.

"How do you know?" asked one of the Heller boys. "Did that boy split your rump with it?"

This triggered genuine laughter from most of the hide hunters.

"And finally that ugly-as-sin greaser down there is called Sangre. He don't say much but rumor has it that one day down in Coahuila he come home to find his woman in bed with another man. He walked up and put his rifle into the man's back and told his woman that if she and the man wanted to be together so bad they could stay together forever. Then he fired that rifle and killed 'em both with one shot, and the man still inside his woman." Kelleren chuckled and shook his head. "But he had to do it that way since he can't see worth a damn 'cept up close. But he sure knows mules and horses and how to get the most out of 'em.".

"So there you have it, Lobo. A rough and rowdy bunch of no-accounts. But one thing you can rely on. They will do what I tell 'em. You know why?"

Riler shook his head.

"Because I'm worse than all of them put together."

"Well then," said Riler, finishing off the whiskey in his cup. "I guess that means I'll have to kill you first if it ever comes to that."

There was a moment of silence as the hide hunters stared at him, and he figured they were trying to determine if he was joking or issuing a threat. But then Kelleren threw back his head and brayed another long, loud belly laugh and his men relaxed.

"God damn it, I like you, Lobo. You ever get tired of living all by your lonesome up in the mountains you should join us. It ain't a bad life, what we do. We go where we want. We do what we want. Just like you've lived your life, I reckon."

"True enough. But, thing is, I don't like crowds." Riler stood up, turned the chair around, and picked up his bottle.

Kelleren leaned forward, elbows on the table, big scarred hands clasped, and looked intently at the mountain man. "How long you aim to stay in Wild Horses, Lobo?"

Riler realized he could go to the blacksmith's right now and saddle his horse and ride on. He had made his trade with Seth Topper, he had all the supplies he needed for another six months at least, and he had visited the Regret. That was all he had intended to do and he had done it all. But he realized right then and there that he wasn't going to be able to leave Wild Horses until Kelleren and his bunch had headed on down the trail to Fort Laramie. Because until that happened then people he liked — Gus and Julie and, of course, Rose — were in jeopardy.

"Long enough," he replied, and with a nod at the hide hunter boss, turned and left the Chinaman's tent saloon by the back way.

          JASON MANNING

CHAPTER 9

When Eldon Caulfield entered the Regret he called out, "Is anyone hurt?" as he rushed to the stairs. He was halfway up when Julie emerged from the dining room.

"Everyone is fine, Mr. Caulfield," she said calmly.

Caulfield came back down the stairs. "I was in the Celestial, heard some of those hide hunters talking about killing Riler. But from what I heard I couldn't figure out what Riler and the man he wounded had quarreled over."

Julie grimaced. She didn't want to relive the moment, but said, "There was one too many hide hunters here this morning. So one of them thought I should see to his ... needs. He took hold of me, and that's when Mr. Riler stepped in."

Caulfield scowled. "If I had been here I would have put a bullet in his brainpan! He had no right to put his hands on you, and for that alone I would have killed him, I assure you!"

"And then his *compadres* would have killed *you*. And maybe others besides you. Riler did the right thing. Out here, Mr. Caulfield, it's Old

Testament. An eye for an eye. Now, I'm sure you are a brave man. But I suggest you avoid those hide hunters while they stay in town."

Caulfield bristled. "I will not walk wide around any man, Mrs. Regret."

Julie sighed and nodded. She had met men like Eldon Caulfield before — men who felt like they always had to prove their manhood. There was no way of knowing why Caulfield had turned out that way. But she had seen plenty of men just like him end up in an early grave.

"Is Rose upstairs?" asked Caulfield.

Julie nodded again. "Most likely in her room. Or maybe with one of the other girls. You can go see her if you like, but I have a feeling those hide hunters will be making tracks through here later today. So please, do what you need to do and then make yourself scarce. Maybe go back to the Celestial." Realizing from the man's expression that he wasn't partial to the notion of being shooed away for his own protection, she tried another tack. "I don't want any more bloodshed in my house, you understand? It's bad for business."

"You do me a grave disservice, Mrs. Regret."

"Let me be frank, sir," she said, grimacing. "I think you care about Rose a little too much, and I will not have you causing a ruckus under my roof because you probably would not be the only person who got hurt if you did. It's likely a good many of those hide hunters will have her in the next day or two, so if that bothers you, then you should leave now rather than later."

Caulfield glared at her but she met his gaze unflinchingly and he finally backed down.

"You have my word as a soldier and a gentleman that I will not cause you or yours any problems whatsoever," he replied, stiffly. He dug a dollar out of his vest pocket and put it in her hand and without another word turned and went up the stairs.

* * *

Caulfield put his ear to the door to Rose's room, and when he heard nothing he knocked, gently. "Rose?" he murmured, hoping he

 JASON MANNING

wouldn't draw the attention of Ana or Molly in their rooms further along the upstairs hallway. "It's Eldon."

There was a squeak of rusty bedsprings and then the door opened and Rose looked at him with red, swollen eyes. For Caulfield, seeing Rose had always been like seeing the sun rise, this beautiful woman-child with her mussed golden took his breath away. His heart seemed to swell in his chest, while passion swirled hot and strong in his loins — as always happened when he laid eye on this girl, even while it occurred to him that she had been crying.

"What's wrong, Rose? Did someone hurt you?" Caulfield thought of Riler, the last man he had seen leaving the brothel. "Was it that mountain man?" he asked, belligerently.

Rose shook her head. It was true, that Riler had hurt her but she wasn't about to try explaining. She had already learned one valuable lesson about men, thanks to her father — that they never really understood a woman's emotions. She didn't dare associate Riler with her tears, afraid that if she did, then Caulfield would run off to confront the mountain man and end up dead.

"No. I'm fine," she said.

"You're not. You've been crying." He took her by the arms. "Tell me, Rose. What's wrong?"

Rose knew what she had to do. She tried to put aside her sadness. She smiled a warm, seductive smile and let go of the quilt and leaned into him, draping slender arms around his neck. She laid her head on his chest and Caulfield put an arm around her and held her close, tenderly stroking her golden hair with the other hand.

"I'm so happy to see you, Eldon," she murmured. "You smell good. Not like those hide hunters. They smell like...pig shit."" She attempted a soft laugh and it sounded genuine. She lifted her head, looked at him with a salacious little curl on her soft full lips, while she let a hand slide down off his shoulder, down over his chest and belly, to the bulge in the crotch of his trousers. "And you're happy to see me, it would seem!"

Caulfield smiled a rakish smile, the desire blazing in his eyes. "In truth I only came here after I heard about what transpired earlier in the day, to make sure everyone was well. But Mrs. Regret talked me out of a dollar and so naturally I came to your door. I hope you don't mind."

She stood there, slender and pale-skinned with her pert young breasts brushing his chest, her hips pressing against his thighs, and looking suddenly bright-eyed and breathless — an expression that endeared her to him.

"Do I look like I mind?"

He stepped into the room, shut the door, and swept her up in his arms, carrying her to the bed and throwing her on it. She sprawled on the saggy mattress, adorned with a tangle of sheet and quilt, and then propped herself up on her elbows, legs akimbo, not carelessly but rather for effect, watching him as he hastily disrobed, laughing softly as he hopped around trying to pull his boots off. "Don't hurt yourself now," she joked. "Should you fall down and knock yourself out I'll be tempted to just roll you over and ride you, and you wouldn't get to feel a thing."

He stared at her. "I think you probably would. You're a shameless hussy, Rose Waldron."

"Why thank you, Sir," she drawled softly.

"You're welcome. It was a compliment."

Then he was on top of her, and inside her, and he groaned with relief while she wrapped her arms and legs around him.

After a few minutes of feverish coupling, his grunts of pleasure mingling with her soft little cries, Caulfield was spent. He rolled off her and lay on his back, chest heaving, and she turned onto her side, head propped on one hand, running the fingers of the other hand through the hair on his chest. He relished the moment of quiet intimacy a moment.

You know," he said, at last, "I've known a few women in my time. But I have never known one who enjoys rogering more than you do, my dear Rose."

"But of course I enjoy it. Why do you think I'm in this line of work?" She laughed.

Caulfield rolled over on his side and propped his head up with his arm. "You haven't told me anything at all about your past," he observed.

Her sultry smile remained in place, but the rest of her lovely face became an emotionless mask. "I'd rather not, is all. I don't care to dwell on the past. I'd rather dream about the future."

I can give you a future," he heard himself say.

Her eyes became hooded and unreadable. "You're not the first man to tell me that."

"I'm quite sure I'm not," he replied. "I expect many are the men who have wanted you for their own." A part of his mind was cautioning him against going further, yet he felt compelled to do just that. "But I mean it, Rose. Ever since I left the Army I've been at loose ends. I wasn't sure what I wanted to do — or be. But now I *am* sure. I want to be your husband. I would give you anything your heart desires. Come with me, away from this room, this town, this life. Come with me to California. I must confess I have...fallen in love with you, Rose."

She tilted her head and studied his face a moment. "You're serious, aren't you?" It was an observation rather than a question.

Caulfield nodded, and grasped her hand in his. "I am. I want to provide for you, to make you happy. From the moment you say yes you'll not have another care in the world."

Rose was silent and thoughtful for a moment, the longest moment in Eldon Caulfield's life. Of a sudden it seemed his life, his future, hinged completely on her answer, that it would be a life worth living or a miserable ordeal depending solely upon her response to his offer. If she accepted he would gain more than just someone to love. To have a wife like Rose would give him purpose, would motivate him to do something with his life and succeed at it so that he would give her everything she deserved and more. It was a motivation he could not seem to muster when he had only his own future to consider.

"Where are you going?" she asked. "San Francisco, perhaps?"

"If you want to live in San Francisco then that is where we'll go, darling."

He could see that she was thinking about it. She was looking around the room, no doubt wondering if she should give up what she knew for the unknown. Caulfield hopes rose. She didn't love him. This he knew and he didn't expect her to. At least not yet. He was no fool. The opportunity to live in a booming city like San Francisco seemed to be of importance to her, which meant his love and attention was not enough to persuade her. He had to wonder if she would be faithful to him. But he decided he would rather live with that than to live without her.

Rose's sultry blue eyes darkened for a moment, as a profound sorrow gripped her again, the first time having been when Lobo Riler left her room earlier that day. But this time it cut deeper as she realized she would have gone anywhere with the mountain man — even up into the high, wild country where he resided. *I should have told him that*, she thought. Then she gave a fierce little shake of her head. *No, it wouldn't have mattered. He doesn't want me. Not like that. Not forever. Just like so many other men, who in the heat of passion thought they had to have me always, but then came to their senses, remembering what I am.* She sighed softly. *I don't deserve a man like Lobo Riler.*

She looked around the room. The room that had been her home for so many months now. A room she had enjoyed, a place of her own. But now it was a place where the mountain man presence remained. She could still see him standing there, looming over her, so tall, so strong, so indomitable, like the mountains he called home. She had felt aroused by the vision, and still felt that way. She ached for how safe she had felt in his presence. She remembered how she had longed to take away the loneliness that pervaded him. She had seen it in his eyes, had heard it in his voice, had felt it in his touch.

But he wasn't going to let her, and suddenly she wanted to escape the sorrow in her heart. The sorrow that this room would harbor as long as she remained in it.

Her sultry blue eyes met Caulfield's again, and a soft, pensive smile touched her lips. "I'll marry you, Eldon."

Elated, Caulfield grabbed and pulled her on top of him, and she tried desperately to put out of her mind the way she had felt in Riler's arms, and then Caulfield was kissing her, a long and passionate kiss.

     JASON MANNING

She had her hands on his chest, pushing gently away, and when his embrace lessened she sat up and rolled off the bed, retrieving her crotchless drawers from the floor.

"We'll have plenty of time for that, Eldon," she murmured. "But let's get out of here. Let's start for San Francisco as soon as possible. Please?"

Caulfield tamped down his desire and nodded. He wanted to believe that her motive for wanting to leave Wild Horses as soon as possible was to avoid a visit from a hide hunter. That was something he devoutly wished, as well.

"I'll go see the Overland man at once and buy our tickets. Come with me."

"But it might be days before another Overland stage comes through. Is there not a way for us to leave sooner? Today? Now?"

Caulfield grimaced as he suddenly had cause to regret all the money he had squandered on himself in his wanderings. He had received a modest sum from the U.S. Army after resigning and had saved a little of his lawman's pay, but nearly all of that was gone now.

"I'll see if I can't buy a horse from him. We may have to ride together."

"I don't care. I just want to leave here."

"Come with me, Rose."

"I should stay, tell Miss Julie the news, and pack my belongings." She bent down and kissed him, her breasts brushing his chest again, by design.

Caulfield dressed hurriedly, and was at the door when he turned to say, "I don't suppose there is anyone in Wild Horses who can marry us? No matter. When we get to San Francisco we'll have a wedding to remember."

She sashayed over to him, naked as the day she had been born, and leaned into him, rising up onto the balls of her feet to kiss him once more. Then she opened the door and said, earnestly. "Hurry back."

Caulfield nodded and left the room, hurried down the stairs and out into the street. The shadows were long, the temperature plunging as the day waned. He walked with long strides down the street, making for the Overland Stage Company's station house.

CHAPTER 10

"You *what?*"

Julie Regret had tired of working in the kitchen. It sometimes seemed to her that she spent her whole life in that room. Now she was standing on the front porch, watching the sun hovering just above a western horizon serrated by distant cobalt-blue mountains while the sky turned pretty shades of pink and orange, when Rose emerged from the cathouse with the surprising news.

Rose repeated herself. "Eldon...Mr. Caulfield ... asked me to marry him and I said yes."

Stunned, Julie stared at the yellow-haired girl. She had crossed paths with plenty of women of easy virtue, and she knew of none who actually relished the work as much as Rose Waldron.

She didn't know a lot about Rose's past. One morning she had just shown up at the door of the Regret. This was a day after a wagon train of emigrants had passed on the Overland Trail and Julie remembered asking Rose if she had been with the wagons, and if she had been accidentally left behind. Rose had said it was no accident, and that was *all* she said about the matter. Many days later, when the subject of family had come up as Julie and the girls sat around the dining room table eating, Rose had said she had a family but they wanted nothing to do with her. Having gotten to know Rose by that time, Julie had already surmised that the westward-bound wagon train had left her behind on purpose. Perhaps her wanton, narcissistic nature had resulted in her being branded a troublemaker that threatened to disrupt the company of pioneers. It was logical to assume that her family had disowned her for the same reason. If a man dallied with another's wife or daughter he could expect to be gunned down. But shooting a wife who cheated on her husband — or a daughter who brought shame upon her family by acting like a harlot — just wasn't done and was rarely forgiven. Instead, the woman was often cast out, divorced, or disowned.

And so Julie Regret was astonished that Rose had agreed to marry. "Are you in love with him?"

Rose shrugged, pretending to be nonchalant. "He's a nice enough man. And he's a very fine lover."

"Well, of course," said Julie, with a derisive and unladylike snort. "So you're *not* in love with him."

"I didn't say I wasn't," replied Rose defensively.

"You didn't say you were, and you would have, if it were so. And you would have that look. The look of a woman in love." She knew that look. She had seen it on her own face, staring into a mirror on the day Moke Regret had proposed to her back in New Orleans.

Julie shook her head and took a deep breath, trying to corral her anger — and to understand it. She wondered why Caulfield hadn't mentioned this development when he emerged from the house a quarter of an hour earlier. He had merely greeted her and rushed on, grinning like a fool and obviously in a hurry. Most men who came out the front door of the Regret were either grinning or smiling or blushing so she hadn't suspected anything out of the ordinary had taken place in Rose's room. Suddenly she felt very sorry for Eldon Caulfield, and now she knew where at least some of her anger was coming from.

"He is going to take me to San Francisco," said Rose. "He's with the Overland man as we speak, arranging our passage. He is going to take care of me, I'm sure. You should be happy for me, Miss Julie."

"He is a decent man and I'm sure he will do right by you," sighed Julie. "But you don't look or sound all that happy to me, Rose. So what's going on here?"

"I just told you," said Rose, clearly on the defensive.

Julie shook her head again. "No, there's something else."

Rose tried to change the subject. "You're just wondering if I will do right by him, aren't you?"

"I won't lie to you. I *am* more than a little skeptical. You don't love him. And believe me, Rose, you have to truly love a man to stand by him in bad times. And there *will* be bad times."

"Like you really loved your husband," said Rose caustically. "You must have, to stick with him in spite of him poking just about every woman who walked by."

Rose instantly regretted her words. She watched Julie warily, expecting the other woman to respond with anger, perhaps even strike her. She saw that anger blaze hot in Julie Regret's eyes, saw the older woman's hands clench into fists. But Julie managed to control herself. She took a deep breath and a long moment to calm herself.

"That's right. I did love him. I loved him enough to overlook even that."

"Oh God," said Rose, in a hushed tone.

Julie realized that Rose wasn't looking at her, but past her and into the street. She looked over her shoulder and her heart lurched in her chest.

Four of the hide hunters had left the Chinaman's tent saloon and were quartering across the street towards the Regret.

Julie didn't hesitate. She took Rose by the arm and rushed her through the doorway and into the cathouse. "You go to your room and you lock the door and you be as quiet as a church mouse, you hear me?"

Rose stared at her, wrenching her arm free and rubbing her arm where Rose had grabbed it. "What are you talking about? I'm just a whore. This is all I'm good for. Isn't that what you were thinking a moment ago?" She shook her head bitterly. "No. I'll do my share just like Molly and Ana. I'll be a good little whore."

"No you will not!" hissed Julie. "Have you already forgotten that you promised to marry Eldon Caulfield? You do what I tell you, Rose, because if you don't someone is likely going to get killed today!"

With that she angrily went back out onto the porch, slamming the door behind her. As she stood at the top of the porch steps, she managed to fasten a friendly smile on her face as the four men arrived. She recognized only one of them — the man who had come rushing downstairs after Riler won his fight with the brute who had entertained thoughts of raping her.

This man grinned up at her. "I'm back, ma'am, seein' as how my fun was interrupted earlier." He gestured at the other three men. "Folks call me Texas Jack. These two here are brothers, Billy and Emmett Heller."

"Emmett and me, we do everything together," drawled Billy, leering. "That includes whores."

Julie glanced at the fourth man, a sullen, stocky black man, who stood with arms folded staring at her, as though expecting her to tell him something he wasn't going to like. Instead, she turned her attention back to Billy Heller.

"I'm afraid that's against house rules," she said, pleasantly. "If you like one of the girls over the others then you will just have to take turns."

"I told you!" crowed Texas Jack, who reeked of cheap whiskey, and looked to be three-sheets into the wind as he wobbled on uncertain legs. "It's on account of that rule ol' Breck got whupped by that mountain man."

"Well hell," said Emmett Ryder, frowning. "That rule don't make no sense. A woman's got more than one hole for pokin'."

Texas Jack took off his hat and walloped Emmett about the head with it. "You mind your manners in front of this lady, swamp trash, 'lessen you want to have to deal with that Riler feller."

"He don't scare me," muttered Emmett, who didn't like being hat-walloped like he was a child.

   Jason Manning

Movement caught out of the corner of her eye made Julie look past them, down the street, and she sighed an "Oh Jesus" when she saw Eldon Caulfield coming back from the Overland house. She held out her hand to the hide hunters.

"That'll be a dollar for each of you."

"Me, too?" asked Morris, his voice pitched low, gruff and resentful. "Weren't sure you allowed your girls to lay with a Negro."

"My girls are whores. The only color we care about here is the color of your money." She was suddenly in a hurry to get the hide hunters inside, and with four dollars in hand she opened the door for them. "For two of you, right up the stairs. Second and third door. The others, please make yourselves comfortable in the parlor on your left. I will bring you a drink, on the house."

Texas Jack glanced at her curiously. "Two? You had three whores earlier."

"One of them is *very* sick. She has been throwing up. Might be something contagious, so I'm keeping her quarantined. But Ana and Molly can take care of all of you." She made a point of looking at Billy Heller as she added, "One at a time."

Rose appeared at the top of the stairs, standing hipshot with her camise unbuttoned, a salacious smile on her moist lips. "Oh, I feel much better now, Miss Julie. I can take one of these big handsome men. Come on up, boys."

"That's the one I want!" shouted Billy Heller, pushing his brother out of the way so he could run up the stairs. Texas Jack and Morris followed him.

Julie watched them, feeling a knot forming in the pit of her stomach. She was furious at Rose, but that anger paled in comparison to the sense of dread that overtook her. And then she looked at Rose just before the first man up the stairs reached her, and was taken aback by the expression on the blonde whore's face. Every other time she was about to be hauled to her room and poked, Rose had looked happy and excited. But not this time. This time she looked resigned to a fate she despised.

At the top of the stairs, Billy Heller and Morris were engaged in a brief exchange of angry words.

"I got dibs on her!" Billy complained.

"You let go of her or I'll snap your scrawny neck," growled Morris.

Billy Heller let go and Morris grabbed Rose and hustled her into her room, kicking the door shut behind him.

Feeling ill-at-ease, Julie managed to compose herself as she escorted Emmett into the parlor. "I'll be back with your drink," she promised, and left the room. Instead of going on through the dining room into the kitchen, she paused and looked anxiously up the stairs and had a sudden urge to go up and somehow get Rose away from the black hide hunter. But then she remembered Caulfield and turned right and slipped out the front door.

Caulfield was only fifty feet away and he was coming on with long strides and a grim expression on his face. He had seen the hide hunters enter the Regret. Now they were under the same roof as his wife-to-be and that he could not tolerate. Julie moved off the porch to intercept him. As she drew near him Julie held her hands out in a slow-down gesture.

"We need to talk, Mr. Caulfield."

"Not right now," he said and started to veer round her.

Julie stepped directly in his path, alarmed by the expression on his face. It was the expression of a man whose most prized possession was in jeopardy of being taken by another — and who intended to do whatever it took to prevent that from happening.

"Yes, right now," she said sternly, grabbing his sleeve and blocking his path. "What do you intend to do?"

He grimaced, too much the gentleman to push her aside or pry her hand off his sleeve. "What do you think, Mrs. Regret?" he snapped. "I intend to get Rose out of there."

She decided not to chastise him for failing to take Rose to the Overland house. That was water under the bridge now, and there was no time to waste. "She has a customer. You'll have to wait until he's done. You wait here on the porch and I will bring her out to you when that happens."

"Let go of my arm, Mrs. Regret," he said coldly.

"You listen to me, Mr. Caulfield, and listen good! Rose Waldron is not your woman yet. So one more man is inside her. Just one more added to the dozens who had gone before him. I realize that isn't something you wish to think about, but those are the facts and you need to swallow your pride and be reasonable. If you go in there now and try to take her away there will be trouble. People will get hurt. Maybe even killed. And one of them might be Rose!"

Caulfield glanced at the cathouse door and then back at her. He was fuming. "You could have told them only Ana and Molly were available."

Julie was about to inform him that she had done just that. But then she would have had to tell him that Rose had disobeyed her and made an appearance — in other words, that Rose had *wanted* one of the hide hunters to poke her, and while it might have been better for Eldon Caulfield to know this in the long run, she just wasn't prepared to damage the man's ego to that extent. He looked so consumed by his passions that she highly doubted such a revelation would cause him to give up on Rose and walk away. Deciding not to defend herself, she let go of his arm and stepped back.

"Unless you don't mind if something bad happens to Rose, you'll stay out here, and I'll bring her out when she's done."

Caulfield looked at the upstairs windows of the house with an anguished expression, then nodded. "Okay. But mark my words, Mrs. Regret. I won't wait long."

Julie hurried inside. Emmett Ryder was still sitting in the parlor, his hat in his lap, chin resting on his chest, and she wasn't sure if he was asleep or not. He and his brother and the others had reeked of whiskey when they had filed past her to come inside, so she clung to the hope that he had fallen into an alcohol-induced slumber. She told herself to go back to the kitchen and wait there, but she was too nervous, and instead paced the hallway, back and forth beside the staircase, praying that in the next few seconds she would hear a door upstairs open and a see a hide hunter coming down the steps. If so, odds were it would be the man who had been with Rose. She was very talented in bed and most men didn't last long with her. Julie thought, *all I have to do is drag her outside and hand her over to Caulfield. Then I'll pack her personal belongings and take it and a little money to wherever he has her stashed away. And then she'll be his problem, and God help him.*

A woman's scream filled the house and turned Julie's blood cold in her veins.

CHAPTER 11

Julie had never heard Rose Waldron scream, but knew it was her. She was halfway up the stairs when the front door of the cathouse burst open with a splintering of wood. It was Caulfield, charging in with his Colt Army Revolver in hand. That made Julie freeze and put her back to the wall because she could also see Emmett Heller jumping to his feet in the parlor, shaken out of his drunken stupor by the scream, his hand closing on the butt of the pistol he carried stuffed under his belt. She watched in horror as Caulfield turned towards the parlor, perhaps catching movement out of the corner of an eye, and he raised the Colt Army as Emmett pulled his smokewagon.

"No." Julie didn't scream it at the two men squaring off down below. She knew it was too late to stop them. It was more of a hoarsely whispered plea for divine intervention. But that didn't happen either.

When Emmett Heller realized Caulfield had the drop on him he hesitated, his pistol only halfway pulled from under his belt. But the expression on Caulfield's face made him realize the other man was going to shoot no matter what, so he kept pulling.

Caulfield knew he had the hide hunter dead to rights. He turned his right side to the man in the parlor, raising his pistol and taking careful aim. His bullet caught Emmett squarely in the chest just as the hide hunter's pistol cleared the belt. That pistol flew out of a dead hand and struck the curtained front window, smashing a pane of glass. Ryder's carcass was knocked backward and he ended up sitting in one of the chairs, arms and legs akimbo. For an instant he seemed to be staring at his killer with eyes full of surprised resentment. But they became sightless eyes, and his head slowly fell forward and once again he looked like he was sleeping.

Caulfield charged up the steps. Julie kept her back to the wall, a hand covering her mouth. It wasn't until he had reached the top of the stairs that she found her voice and shouted, "For God's sake don't go up there!" But Caulfield didn't seem to hear her. He didn't look at all like the smiling, sophisticated, handsome man she knew, but rather like a wild animal out for blood.

He was at the top of the stairs and taking the first step towards the door to Rose's bedroom when a door down the hall flew open, cracking back on its hinges, and Texas Jack came out wearing only grimy long johns, a pistol in hand. Caulfield began to turn in that direction, bringing his pistol around. An instant later the door to Rose's room was flung open and Caulfield caught a glimpse of Morris. The big bare-chested black man had a butcher knife clutched in his hand. Before Caulfield could shoot him, Texas Jack got off a shot from the other end of the upstairs hall. The bullet caught Caulfield high in the shoulder. It felt like he had been hit with a heavy, hard-swung pole. The impact knocked him into the door frame and he would have gone down in the hall if Morris hadn't grabbed him and driven the knife into his belly. He felt a lancing pain in his midsection, so intense it knocked the wind out of him. Then he was yanked forward into the room, losing his balance and sprawling on the floor. He managed to roll over and looked up at the looming teamster, who was grinning down at him.

In that moment he knew he was going to die.

"All I wanted was a lock of the bitch's hair," said Morris, "but she

    Jason Manning

didn't want me to have it. So I took it and then some."

He held up long strands of blonde curls tangled in his fingers.

Caulfield stared at the strands of hair and felt sick. "Rose!" he croaked, and then tried to get up but his hands slipped out from under him. They were covered with blood — his own blood, which was pooling on the floor. Still, he tried to crawl towards the bed. "Oh God, no!" he gasped, his voice high and reedy. "Rose! ROSE!"

Chuckling, Morris stepped over him and went around to the side of the bed. "She ain't dead, boss. But maybe she ain't quite as purdy as she used to be."

Caulfield rolled over on his back. The room was beginning to spin and tilt and he tasted bile and thought he was going to throw up. He heard the old bed springs squall in complaint, and then he saw Rose, or at least Rose from the shoulders up. She was looking down at him with tears running down her cheeks. Morris had cut a fistful of her hair off close to the scalp on the right side of her head, and in the process had cut her ear, separating the top part, the helix, from her head. Blood was streaming down her face and neck, onto her shoulder and a rivulet made its way down the curve of her bare breast. Rose's tears and her blood rained down on Caulfield's face.

Texas Jack appeared in the doorway and stared at the scene a moment. Caulfield tried to raise the Army Colt but it suddenly felt like it weighed fifty pounds. Texas Jack shut the door behind him and stepped forward to kick the Army Colt out of Caulfield's hand. It skittered across the floor and under the bed.

"What the hell have you done, Morris?" shouted Texas Jack, angrily. "You done ruined the prettiest whore in town and you know there ain't many pretty whores around!"

Morris shrugged and tossed Rose away. She sprawled on the bed and cowered against the headboard with the stunned look of prey on her face, hugging herself tightly and trembling violently.

"Don't matter none," said Morris calmly. "I wanted me something to remember her by, is all."

"Well, you gave her something to remember *you* by, that's for sure and certain." Texas Jack looked down at Caulfield, aimed his pistol at him, then shook his head. "Looks like you gutted this one real good. No point in wasting a bullet. He'll bleed out."

A strangled shout of rage mixed with anguish came from downstairs.

"Sounds like Billy," said Texas Jack, and left the room in a hurry. Morris stuck the knife under his belt, grabbed his shirt off the back of a chair, and gave Rose an indifferent glance before following.

Billy had gone downstairs and into the parlor to find his brother's body. He was standing there, shaking, staring at Emmett's corpse sprawled in the chair, the front of his shirt dark and soaked with blood.

Texas Jack took a quick look back through the hall into the dining room, wondering where Julie Regret was. Then he heard her, outside, shouting.

"Riler! RILER, WHERE ARE YOU?"

Texas Jack felt a chill dance down his spine. He took hold of Billy and pushed him towards the door ahead of him. "Let's get of here. We need to tell Kelleren what's happened."

"What about him?" asked Morris, gesturing at Emmett's body.

"Leave him for now. I got a feelin' we'll have more than one dead man to bury today."

* * *

After enjoying a nice hot bath in a tent behind the Celestial, attended to by Woo's wife, who kept the bath steaming hot with buckets of water heated over an open fire, Riler got dressed and paid her for what was, for him, a rare indulgence, one he looked forward to every time he came to Wild Horses. There were a couple of spring-fed mountain creeks up near his cabin where he generally washed himself every fortnight or so, even in wintertime, but to lay back and soak in warm water was a real pleasure.

Slinging his shot pouch over one shoulder and slanting his Sharps over the other, he emerged from the tent and looked into the larger tent where Woo had his saloon. He noted the lengthening shadows — the day was nearly done, the sun nearly touching the jagged peaks of the high country to the west, and he was thinking about Rose and weighing his options. He could spend the night at Gus Freeman's smithy, or ride out of town a few miles and make camp — or he could return to the brothel and spend the night with Rose. He paused there in a moment of indecision that was rare for him.

Kelleren and some of his men were still at the tables under the big tent, still drinking, still talking and laughing, but he didn't pay them much attention, his thoughts on the slender blonde whore and how much he wanted to lay with her again and how guilty he felt as a result, because every time he thought about Rose Waldron he saw an image of Quahneah in his mind's eyes and he was plagued with a powerful guilt.

He wasn't sure what he would do but he knew he didn't want to talk to the hide hunters again, so he was starting round the back corner of the tent saloon, heading towards the town's single street when he heard a woman's blood-curdling scream followed by a gunshot. He stopped; trying to gauge which direction the sounds had come from. For an instant the town of Wild Horses seemed to hold its breath — even the tent saloon had fallen silently. Less than a minute later there was another gunshot, and now Riler knew it came from the general direction of the brothel, and then it occurred to him that there wasn't a full contingent of hide hunters in the Celestial because some of them were probably at Julie Regret's place. He walked with long strides for the street. He reached it just as Kelleren and six other hide hunters came boiling out of the Celestial, weapons in hand, looking all around — until Riler came into view. Then they all looked at him.

A heartbeat later Julie Regret came boiling out of the whorehouse, calling his name.

"Damn," he muttered, and swung the Sharps down off his shoulder. There was already a sheared paper cartridge in the breech, so all he had to do was pull the hammer back. The Navy Revolver remained under his belt. While it was fully loaded — six .36 caliber Minie balls with twenty grains of powder in a tapered paper cartridge — and handy enough in close quarters, as a street fight likely would be, he still preferred his long gun for stopping power. He walked out into the street, pivoting as he moved so that he could face the hide hunters. He wasn't aiming the Sharps at anyone but he was watching Kelleren and every one of his men, and at the same time throwing up a hand, palm out, in Julie's direction. "Stop right there!" he called out, wanting to keep her out of the line of fire should shooting erupt.

Kelleren was scowling and he took a step forward, hands balled into fists, dark piggish eyes blazing. "What's going on?" he shouted at Riler, and then, to Julie, "What the hell's going on at your place?"

Riler brought the Sharps to shoulder, aiming it at Kelleren. "Stand back," he warned. He threw a quick glanced over his right shoulder to see that Julie had come to a halt.

And then Texas Jack emerged from the Regret with Billy Heller and Morris and upon seeing the other hide hunters bunched up in front of the Celestial Billy shouted, choking on emotion, "My brother's dead! Emmett's been kilt!"

Julie spun around, saw the three men on her porch and then saw the strands of golden hair dangling from the black man's fist and her stomach did a slow roll. Her hands flew to her face and she gasped "Oh dear God in heaven!"

Realizing that Riler was in the middle of the street, aiming his rifle at Kelleren, Billy Heller grabbed for the pistol at his side. Texas Jack tried to latch onto him, and Billy assumed it was to try and stop him. But he violently shrugged off his fellow hunter and sidestepped, raising the pistol and drawing a bead on the mountain man.

Riler accepted then that he was probably going to be shot, and most likely killed— but it wasn't going to be by Billy Heller, the man Kelleren had introduced as a crack shot with rifle or pistol. He swung ninety degrees to his right, the butt of the breechloader remaining snug against his shoulder, instinctually turning the right side of his body even more, providing Billy with less of a target, and pulled the trigger. The hammer fell, throwing one of the twenty-odd primer pellets stored in a small magazine below the hammer onto the nipple an instant before the hammer dropped. The Sharps bucked against his shoulder and he felt the heat of the gas discharge on the inside of his right wrist, the 36-inch barrel burping a puff of acrid gun smoke.

     JASON MANNING

He was already moving before the .52 caliber traveled the hundred and fifty feet and lodged itself in the skull of Billy Heller, entering right above the bridge of his nose, killing him instantly. The impact threw the hide hunter abruptly backwards, knocking him off his feet. While moving, Riler levered the breech block down, fished a paper cartridge out of his shot pouch, shoved it into the breech, pulled the lever back so that the block sheered the paper off the backside of the cartridge, and cocked the hammer — all in the handful of seconds it took him to reach Julie, who stood trembling and apparently paralyzed with fear in the middle of the street about ten long strides away. He could load and fire the Sharps five times in about a minute.

In the time it took Riler to reach Julie, the hide hunters congregating with Kelleren in front of the Celestial didn't move, and instead were staring at Billy Heller going down. But then they reacted, scattering and filling their hands with shooting iron.

Riler hooked an arm 'round Julie's waist and swept her off her feet, turning sharply to the right as he did so and making for the nearest alley between the two clapboard buildings due east of the Regret, in this way hoping to get her out from the middle of the gunfire he expected to erupt any second. The next building down was Seth Topper's, and just as Riler turned he saw the trading post door open and Topper emerge with his double-barreled, sawed-off shotgun. Dohasan came out right behind him, grabbing Topper's arm and trying to stop him and pull him back inside. Further down the street was the wolf-dog, a blur of black and gray fur running full-tilt right for Riler. When his master was in peril no command was going to keep him rooted in place.

On the brothel porch, Texas Jack stood staring down at the corpse of Billy Heller and saw a little rivulet of dark red blood emerging from the gaping black hole in the dead man's forehead. Billy had died so quickly he still wore the expression of grief-stricken fury he had worn when he drew on the mountain man. Then Texas Jack saw movement out of the corner of his eye. It was Morris, hastening back inside the whorehouse. Only then did Texas Jack draw his pistol and aim it at Lobo Riler. But he hesitated when he saw that Julie Regret was with the mountain man. Unlike some of his hide hunting companions, he didn't cotton to the idea of shooting a woman.

The buckskin-clad sharpshooter named Jim Early didn't hesitate, though. He was the first to draw a bead on Riler, and he was too good of a marksman to worry about hitting Julie Regret.

Riler was counting the seconds and his strides, and when he reached five he was about to push Julie down and try to shield her with his body when the 58-caliber Minie ball hit him and knocked him down. He lost his grip on Julie and hit the hardpack in such a way that he nearly blacked out. For a few seconds he simply felt numb. Then the pain came, an explosion of excruciating pain that took his breath away. He managed to lift his head and saw that Julie, who had stumbled and nearly lost her balance when he went down, was now turning towards him. He tried to shout at her to "Run!" but all he could produce was an incoherent grunt. His vision was darkening and then he was spiraling down into a black pit of unconsciousness.

"I got him!" crowed Jim Early, as he began to reload the Springfield.

"I'll fetch his scalp!" called out McNally, brandishing one of his long knives and starting off across the street. He was focused on the fallen mountain man and didn't see Seth Topper in the deepening shadows beneath the trading post's porch roof until Topper, having shaken Dohasan loose, circled around the hide-laden wagons. Kelleren had left them parked in front because they would be easy to keep an eye on from the Chinaman's watering hole, which was almost directly across the street. As soon as he had come out into the street and had a clear shot, Topper triggered one barrel of the ten-gauge. Some of the buckshot kicked up dust around McNally's feet, but most of it hit him in both legs, knocking him down.

Topper looked bleakly at Riler laying face-down in the street, just as Julie Regret, sobbing and disconsolate, fell to her knees beside the mountain man. Then the trader turned his attention — and his shotgun — on Kelleren and the four men who stood near him in front of the Celestial, and angrily shouted, "You scurvy sons of bitches!"

McNally was in the middle of street yowling for help, writhing as

     Jason Manning

he grabbed at his buckshot-peppered legs, but none of the hide hunters were paying him any mind. They were focused on Topper, and two of them, Jim Early and Jonah Johnson, fired at him before he could cut loose with the second barrel of buckshot. Johnson fired his old dragoon pistol first and the ball hit Topper high in the chest and spun him around, and he caught a glimpse of Dohasan, standing in the partial shelter of one of the wagons, staring at him in horror. It was the last thing Seth Topper saw as Jack Early's Springfield rifle barked and the Minie ball hit him dead square. The trader hit the hardpack of the street, limp as a rag doll, the shotgun slipping out of lifeless fingers and hitting the street halfway between Dohasan and his adopted father's corpse.

Kelleren was standing well back from the other hide hunters, keeping them between him and the street. When he saw Topper go down he pushed forward, noticed McNally writhing in the dust and grumbled to the mute Dakota Sioux, "Chaytan, go get Mac out of the street." He glanced in the direction of the Regret and saw that Texas Jack was on one knee beside Billy Heller. Kelleren assumed Billy was dead because Lobo Riler had shot him. He also assumed that Texas Jack was rifling through the pockets of the dead man to see if there was anything of value. He was wondering where Morris had run off to — he hadn't see the black teamster go back inside the Regret — when Jonah Johnson hollered "Look out!" and caught a glimpse of the wolf-dog running up to the mountain man face down in the dirt. When he pulled a pistol out of his belt the wolf-dog stopped whining and sniffing at the mountain man's body and looked around, then lowered its head, ears back and fangs bared, crouching in an attack stance over its master.

"Mean as hell," muttered Kelleren, with a slow grin. "Just like its owner."

In that instant Dohasan broke from the cover of the hide wagons, grabbed Topper's scattergun, and then threw himself behind the body of the dead trader. He placed a trembling hand on the dead trader's arm and whispered, "*Ah-lay*. Father," following the Dakota word for the English one, as Topper had taught him to do.

Jonah Johnson had seen Dohasan make his play for the shotgun, but by the time he started firing his pistol in that direction the Dakota youth had already sheltered behind the body. Johnson sometimes forgot to close his lazy eye when he got excited, and he was excited now, so he was seeing double and his first shots went high and the next two kicked up spurts of dust a few feet shy of the trapper's corpse and then he closed his bad eye and his fifth bullet thunked into the trader's body.

When he heard the bullet thump into his white father's body, Dohasan lay the shotgun across Topper's body, shouting *"Mah ting-tee!"* DIE!" and triggered the second barrel at the cluster of men in front of the tent saloon. The range was over a hundred feet and the buckshot was losing its velocity and scattering when it reached Kelleren and his crew. A pellet hit Johnson in the hand and he dropped his pistol and howled and hopped, shaking his hand violently, like he thought he could shake the pain away. Kelleren was hit high in the right arm and another grazed his neck and he forgot all about Riler's wolf-dog and, along with the rest of the hide hunters, scrambled for whatever shelter the Celestial offered. Johnson and Early turned left and dropped behind the half-wall of logs on that side, while Sangre and Kelleren ducked down on the other side of the entrance. The latter muttered a curse as he put a hand on his neck and then looked at it and saw it smeared with his blood. He scanned the interior of the tent saloon and could see from his vantage point that there was no one skulking behind the bar. the Chinaman and most likely his entire family had disappeared at the first sign of trouble.

"Sangre," he growled, "you and Early go out the back way and circle around and get those damned wagons turned around."

"*Si, jefe*," said the Mexican. He pushed away from the half-wall and hurried out the back of the tent, followed by the buckskin-clad sharpshooter.

"God damn!" God damn!" wailed Johnson. "I'm shot and I dropped my pistol."

"Don't matter," gruffed Kelleren. "You're maybe the worst damn pistol shot I ever did see, next to Sangre."

"I hit that trader!"

"Even a blind squirrel finds a nut every now and then."

Still sheltering behind the corpse of his adoptive father, Dohasan searched Topper's trouser pockets, found several more shells and laid them on the hardpack beside him. He broke open the scattergun, plucked the spent cartridges out of the barrels then picked up one of the new shells and shook it next to his ear before loading it. He did likewise with a second one. It was something else his white father had taught him, to make sure the shells were good before loading them. As he was closing the ten-gauge he saw Chaytan come running out of the Celestial, evidently heading for the wounded hide hunter.

As Chaytan neared the wounded skinner he noticed that the woman kneeling near Riler's body was tugging a Navy Revolver out of the mountain man's belt. At the same time the wolfdog guarding its master's body was crouched and snarling a warning in his direction. The sound and the fact that the beast's body was coiled like a spring, the Sioux felt his nape hair stand on end. He hauled McNally to his feet and turned for the Chinaman's tent saloon. But McNally took a couple of shuffling steps and then dropped to his knees, obviously in excruciating pain, and Chaytan left him then because a backward glance informed him that Julie was bringing Riler's pistol around to bear. He zigged and zagged and then threw himself into the saloon, hoping he would hear the gunshot. It was the one you didn't hear that killed you.

But Julie Regret didn't shoot. Despite the situation there was something inside her that rebelled against shooting a man in the back. So she sat there beside Riler, glancing at the large black and gray wolf-dog that now lay draped across the mountain man, and wondered, too, why it wasn't snarling at her. An instant later the wolf bared its fangs and a menacing rumble welled up from its throat and Julie cringed — and then realized the beast wasn't looking at her but past her. She looked over her shoulder, alarmed, and breathed a sigh of relief when she saw Gus Freeman coming up the alley towards her.

Gus stopped in his tracks as he heard the wolf-dog's growl, throwing out his hands and stammering, "Easy now. Easy now! Mrs. Regret, you hurt?"

"No. Come help me pull Riler out of the street!"

"No, ma'am! I ain't coming anywhere near that wolf, and long as he's lying like he is, ain't nobody moving Lobo."

Julie saw two men emerge onto the street from around the side of the Chinaman's big tent. They ran for the wagons parked in front of Topper's trading post. She was reluctant to leave Riler's side, even though she wasn't sure if he was alive or dead. She felt responsible for his laying there bleeding.

Dohasan saw Sangre and Early appear in the street when Julie did, and he realized that when they reached the wagons — the nearest one was not thirty feet behind him — he could be caught in a crossfire. He calculated his chances of getting inside the trading post, and decided they were slim or none, and without a second thought he was up and sprinting down the alley on the west side of the post.

Kelleren was keeping an eye on Dohasan — or rather on Topper's corpse, since the Indian boy was doing a fine job of hiding behind it — and when Dohasan suddenly leaped to his feet and sprinted down the alley he got off a single shot, which missed, since moving his wounded right arm caused him considerable discomfort. The kick of the pistol in his grip vibrated up his arm and caused him even more, to the point that he cursed a blue streak and transferred the pistol to his left hand which he knew made him about as useful at slinging lead as Jonah Johnson.

Reaching the wagons, Early and Sangre climbed up into the boxes, gathered up the reins and hurrahed the mule teams into motion, trailing the horses tethered to the back of each wagon. Wild Horses' single street was wide enough to turn a wagon around, and they managed to do just that, pulling up in front of the Celestial.

On the other side, Gus Freeman saw the wagons on the move, and he also saw Julie Regret latching onto one of Lobo Riler's arms and trying to drag him back into the alley. She wasn't making much progress. Just standing there watching made Gus feel guilty, so he managed to put aside his fear — the fear of being shot as well as the fear of being attacked by the wolf-dog, who had gotten up as soon as Julie started trying to move its master. Gus grabbed the mountain man's other arm, wondering if it was worth the risk, since he couldn't tell if Riler was still alive, but Julie was determined to pull him out of the street.

Being wounded, Jonah Johnson managed to get himself onto the bench of the second wagon, driven by Early, and for the same reason Kelleren got up on the lead wagon, while Chaytan untied his Indian pony and vaulted aboard the animal, then rode up alongside the first wagon.

"Take Breck's horse to him. If he's conscious he can try to ride with us." Kelleren didn't think that would be the case, since Breck had a broken nose and possibly a cracked skull, apart from the knife wound Riler had inflicted. "If he ain't, leave his horse. We're gettin' the hell out of here."

Chaytan nodded, collected Breck's horse, and rode down alongside the big tent saloon, making for one of the smaller tents out back, where Breck was laid up.

Kelleren bent forward to look past Sangre and across the street, to see that Julie Regret and a black man he didn't know dragging Riler into an alley, followed by the wolf-dog.

"*Crees que está muerto?*" asked Sangre.

"Don't know," huffed Kelleren. "Right now that damn Injun kid worries me more. And might be others in this town to worry about, too. So let's get a move on."

McNally had dragged himself across the hardpack once the wagon's stopped in front of the Chinaman's place, and he was trying to climb up the right-side fender, managing to get one leg under him but unable to lift the other to put booted foot into stirrup. Seeing this, Sangre jumped down out of the box and went back to lend a hand, hoisting the wounded skinner into the worn hull strapped to the back of his pony.

Bent over his saddlehorn, pale and grimacing, McNally groaned, "I'm in a world of hurt, *compadre*."

"*Puedes quedarte aquí y morir. Entonces no más dolor,*" replied Sangre, with apparent disinterest, then climbed back up into the box using the right front wheel of the wagon.

As the wagons began to move, Texas Jack left the brothel's porch and got his horse detached from the second wagon and swung into the saddle. "What about Billy's and Emmett's horse?" He called out.

"Maybe we'll sell 'em to the cavalry," shouted Kelleren. "We're headin' for Fort Laramie, boys."

They were nearly past the Regret when Morris came out the front door, dragging the yellow-haired whore, who was clutching at the throat an old quilt wrapped loosely around her otherwise naked body, who was stumbling along behind without much fight left in her. Kelleren motioned for Sangre to stop the wagon and the Mexican climbed the leathers threaded through his fingers.

Morris came around to Kelleren's side. "Thought mebbe we was leavin' town," he said. "Thought mebbe we could bring the whores with us. But cain't find them other two. Just this one. She be the purdiest one anyhow."

"I ought to kill you where you stand, you son of a bitch," growled Kelleren. He looked at Rose's bleeding scalp, then fastened cold beady eyes on the black teamster. "You started all this."

Morris was afraid, and showed it. He shook his head. "No, suh, I didn't start nothin'. That feller what talks like a book, he kilt Emmett and came bargin' in the room and might've kilt me but Texas Jack shot him first."

Kelleren made an angry, dismissive gesture. "Get on your cayuse, you dumb son of a bitch" he muttered, and then, to Sangre, "Move out!"

Having succeeded in getting Riler out of the street, Julie's attention was drawn to the sound of wagons on the move, and went back up the alley and peered round the corner of the building. She saw Morris on a horse with Rose Waldron's body draped face down across the saddle in front of him, what was left of the hair on her head dangling, while she clutched the saddle. Morris yanked the quilt off of her and let it flutter to the ground.

"Oh Dear God no!" breathed Julie, horrified, and was about to run into the street when Gus Freeman grabbed her by the arm and pulled her back.

"Ain't a thing you can do to help that gal now, Mrs. Regret," he said grimly. "'Lessen you want to end up like her, you'd best stay put. Only one person I know could get her back." He looked down at Lobo Riler.

Julie looked at the blacksmith then at Riler, tears leaving a wet trail through the dust caked on her cheeks. "Is he even alive?"

Gus nodded. "Barely."

CHAPTER 12

As the hide hunter wagons trundled out of Wild Horses, surrounded by the four horsemen, the riderless mounts and the packhorse, Julie broke into a run, making for the Regret, her concern in that moment the fate of Ana and Molly. Stepping wide around the corpse of Billy Heller, whose head rested in a pool of blood, she went through the opened front door. She checked every room downstairs first, but the only person on that level was Emmett Heller, lying dead in the parlor. She went upstairs and peered into the charnel house that was Rose's room — the blood-spattered sheets and another pool of blood on the floor and the bloodied clothes on Eldon Caulfield's body. Assuming he was dead, she turned and stumbled down the hall, trying desperately not to throw up, calling out the names of the other two whores in a strangled voice. The doors to their rooms were open and she checked under each bed. Then she checked her own room but it too was empty.

 Jason Manning

She had expected to find them dead, and even though she was weeping inconsolably she clung to the hope that they weren't as she hurried clumsily down the stairs and through the dining room and the kitchen, emerging from the house through the back door and screaming Ana's and Molly's names.

Then the smokehouse door creaked open on rusty hinges and the two women she was looking for ventured out. Clinging to one another, they looked around fearfully, and she ran to them and wrapped her arms around them.

"Rose," sobbed Molly. "Is … is Rose still alive?"

Julie nodded, tried to fix a reassuring smile on her quivering lips even as she began to weep convulsively. That was enough to make Molly even more anxious.

"Where is she? Mrs. Julie, WHERE IS SHE?"

'They took her, Molly. They took her."

"NO!" wailed the other woman.

"Que Dios tenga misericordia de ella!" whispered Ana, crossing herself.

Julie herded them inside, sat them at the table in the kitchen, and lit a lamp, as the last remnant of daylight was fading away in the western sky. Then she stiffened and looked up, alarmed, as she heard boots in the front hall. Gus and Topper's Indian son appeared, laboring to put Riler on the dining room table, and an amazed Gus looked over her shoulder at him and said, "He's alive! Somehow he's still alive."

Entering the dining room, Julie looked down at the mountain man. The bottom half of his deerskin shirt was black and glistening with blood. She saw the ragged hole the Minie ball had made in front — the slug had passed through the fleshy part of his upper torso, below the ribcage and above the hip, and exited.

A sudden calm overtook her. Many were the times she had been required to tend to Moke, who had been injury prone, with some of those injuries quite serious. She saw Aba in the kitchen doorway and said, "We're going to need a lot of water, a lot of clean cloth. Get all the clean sheets out the wardrobe in my room. And we'll need hot iron. Stoke the fire in the stove." She turned back to the table and saw Gus using a knife to carefully cut and saw through the tough deerskin of Riler's shirt, so Julie looked at Dohasan.

"Seth...Mr. Topper...is he....?"

Dohasan's face was a stoic mask, but his eyes glistened and his Adam's apple was bobbing as he replied, his voice husky with emotion. "Dead."

"Oh! I am so sorry!" Distraught, she shook her head. "So much death....so suddenly..."

"It's not over," said Dohasan coldly. "One of those men is still here in town. The big one I saw carried out of this house earlier."

Julie remembered then, the man who had thought to rape her, the one Riler had wounded. Had that been today? It seemed to her that this had to be the longest day of her life.

Dohasan was heading for the front door.

"Where are you going?" asked Julie. The look the Indian lad gave her right before he left the house answered her question.

* * *

Dohasan had left the ten-gauge tilted against a wall in the alley where he had found Gus and Riler, and he retrieved it now, returning to the trading post. Going behind the counter he paused and looked round with bleak eyes. This store had been his home for the last half-dozen years. But now it didn't feel like home anymore. It was already a place with too many memories for him to ever feel comfortable in again.

He swiped at his eyes and found some shells for the shotgun under the counter and went out onto the porch. A vivid memory made him pull up short. He had first laid eyes on Seth Topper on this porch, as the trader had come out to greet Dohasan's Sioux father, while his mother stood out in the street with him, an arm around his shoulders. It was then that the deal had been struck, when he had been given to the trader in exchange for a horse to replace the one his Sioux father had lost to a mountain lion days before. He remembered his Sioux father having to pull him free of his weeping mother's grasp, remembered knowing that his mother's *hijgnaku* truly believed it was the right thing to do, so that Dohasan did not have to share the shame and

 JASON MANNING

banishment his mother had brought down upon them by her flagrant promiscuity.

Gazing at Seth Topper's body a moment, blinking as tears defeated his attempts to clear his vision, Dohasan was torn between the need to strike out and the thought that he should get the body out of the street. Then he considered what his white father would have done had their situations been reversed — and with fierce strides he crossed the street and headed down the alley alongside the Chinaman's tent saloon.

He knew where the hide hunter named Breck had been taken after his run-in with Lobo Riler. Earlier that day, shouts from the street had brought him out of the trading post to investigate, in time to see some of Kelleren's men carrying one of their own from the Regret to the Celestial. Topper had joined him, commenting grimly that it looked like one of those "scurvy ruffians" had run into Riler, and that soon there would be hell to pay, then told Dohasan to go to the whorehouse and make sure his old friend was still "above snakes." After being greeted at the back door by Riler, he had taken a detour, across the street and around behind the big tent saloon, to spot the wounded hide-hunter in one of the smaller tents behind the Celestial, laid up in one of the cots the Chinaman rented out to travelers who needed a place to sleep.

When he came around the back corner of the big tent he stopped in his tracks. The burly hide hunter named Breck was gripping the reins of the sorrel horse that Chaytan had left with him, as though about to climb into the saddle. But he couldn't. He was unable to raise his left leg high enough, or bend the knee enough to fit boot into stirrup, and he was cursing a blue streak. Standing near at hand, Mr. Woo was saying, "But you owe money. None of your friends paid me!" Woo's wife and one of her children, a boy younger than Dohasan, stood nearby as spectators.

It was the wife who noticed Dohasan first. Her eyes widened, fear registering on her face, and she cried out something in Chinese as she pointed at him. Breck spun around and planted his injured leg poorly, grimacing as it almost gave way under him, while his hand closed round the butt of a pistol in his belt.

Dohasan didn't hesitate. He triggered one barrel at a distance of no more than twenty feet. The buckshot struck Breck in the chest. The sorrel, whinnied shrilly as it reared. Stepping closer, Dohasan noticed that the hide hunter wasn't quite dead. He thumbed the shotgun's second trigger back and fired at point-black range. Woo's wife screamed, trying to cover her boy's eyes. The sorrel began to spin around, intent on galloping away, but Dohasan was quick — he lunged and grabbed the trailing reins, dropping the empty ten-gauge and using both hands to hold onto the leathers as the horse tried to rear again. Horse-talking in Sioux, he soon had the sorrel calmed. He looked down at the man he had killed without remorse, then, with a glance at Woo, turned to lead the horse away.

"Wait!" said Woo. "I keep horse! This man and his friends did not pay me."

Dohasan shook his head. "I need him."

"No," said Woo. "It belongs me."

"No," snarled Dohasan. "That isn't the man who killed my father. I am going after the one who did."

He continued on his way, leading the horse around the corner of the tent and back to the street.

* * *

Julie Regret worked for about an hour on Lobo Riler before she began to think he might actually survive. It wasn't the wound itself but the amount of blood that the mountain man had lost that most alarmed her.

Before she went to work she sent Gus Freeman upstairs to check on Eldon Caulfield. The blacksmith came back with word that Caulfield was, indeed, dead. "Looks like he done bled out."

Julie sighed, deeply saddened. "I suspect the last thing he saw before he died was Rose, bleeding and at the mercy of that son of a bitch who nearly scalped her."

"He was sweet on her or something?"

Julie nodded. "Asked her to marry him."

Gus was silent a moment, rubbing his chin, pondering her words, then shook his head. "She was purdy enough, I reckon, but I sure wouldn't fall in love with a whore. No offense, Miss Julie."

"You said 'was'."

"Beg pardon?"

"You said Rose *was* pretty enough."

Gus mumbled an apology.

"Truth is, some men feel the need to be knights in shining armor," said Julie, more to herself than to the others in the room. "He no doubt thought Rose was a lady trapped by circumstance into selling her body. That's not true, you know. That's not true of any whore I've ever met." She glanced at the inscrutable Ana, standing quietly in the kitchen doorway. "Rose enjoys being with men. I suspect that's why she ended up on my doorstep. I don't profess to know why some women turn out that way, but I know it's true." She sighed. "Maybe they hate themselves. Maybe they think that's all they're good for."

She glanced at the inscrutable Ana, standing quietly in the kitchen doorway. "Go stir up the fire in the stove. Put some water on to boil. Put the iron in the fire and leave it there until it's red-hot." She referred to an iron poker she used to stir up the fire in the potbelly stove.

The first task of course was to stop the bleeding. After trying to clean around each bullet hole with a damp cloth, she opted for trying gunpowder first, sending Molly down to the general store to fetch some, since she didn't keep that sort of thing around the house. While she waited for this, continuing to try to stifle the flow of blood from the exit wound, she heard a distant gunshot, followed in close order by another.

"Sounded like a shotgun," said Gus, parting the chintz drapes that covered the room's front window to look out at the street. "Probably Ol' Seth's ten-gauge."

Julie nodded. "I guess that means one less hide hunter. Good riddance."

"What are we going to do about Rose, *señora?*" asked Ana.

Julie sighed, shook her head and closed her eyes as the vision of

Rose Waldron draped over that black hide hunter's saddle came to mind. She figured it was an image that was going to be indelibly imprinted on her mind.

"Once we've done all we can for Mr. Riler I guess I'll go try to get her back."

"That's plumb crazy," said Gus. "Beggin' your pardon, miss. Reckon you can kill all eight of those men?" He had counted Kelleren's crew when they had arrived in Wild Horses. Two of them were laying down here at the brothel and he assumed Dohasan had just killed a third. "'Cause that's how many you'll have to kill to get her back. More likely you'll end up just like her. And how is that gonna help her?"

"What do you want me to do?" she snapped. "Just sit here and do nothing?"

Gus looked grimly at the unconscious mountain man sprawled face-up on the bloodied dining room table.

"Let *him* do it."

"Did you not notice how serious is his wound? It will be weeks before he can ride again. And I...." Tears suddenly welled up in her eyes and she swiped angrily at them with the back of her blood-stained hands. "And I can only imagine what those men will do to Rose in that time."

Pouring about fifty grains of powder into both the entry and exit holes, she had Gus and Ana and Molly hold Riler down as she struck a lucifer on the edge of the dining room table and set flame to powder. The flare of ignition was followed by the smell of scorched flesh, and while the entry hole stopped dripping blood the exit hole didn't, and she had to resort to the iron poker. The sizzling sound of the red-hot iron on flesh nauseated her, but she kept at it until the bleeding was well and truly stopped. Through it all, Riler moaned and moved some, but remained unconscious, and she was grateful for that.

While this was going on, several strips of cloth had been steeped in water boiling in a big pan set on the kitchen stove. Ana fetched them on a big two-pronged fork and carried them this way out the back door, to throw them over the clothes line that stretched from a back

   Jason Manning

corner of the house to a stout six-foot cedar post driven into the ground. Night had fallen and a cold wind buffeted the wet cloths. Ana went back inside.

"*Que se seca pronto, señora,*" she said as she returned dining room.

Julie had collapsed exhausted into a chair. She nodded. "*Gracias,* Ana." She glanced through the chintz curtains and saw that darkness had descended on Wild Horses. This made her think about Rose, and what Rose would have to endure this night. She abruptly leaned forward, elbows on her knees, face in her hands, and began sobbing loudly.

Gus glanced at Ana and Molly, then walked around the table and put what was intended to be a comforting hand on Julie's shuddering shoulder.

"Don't you worry so, Miss Julie," he said. "All that girl has got to do is want to stay alive no matter what happens. Stay alive long enough for Lobo here to find her."

"What makes you think she's like that?" asked Julie.

Gus shrugged. "I don't rightly know that she is. But I do know I ain't particularly strong-willed myself, but I survived a pretty had time. I 'member it like it was yesterday. I 'member how one day I decided that I was going to *live*! No matter how hard they worked me, or how little they fed me … or how hard they beat me. So I know if I could do it, anyone can. If they want to."

Julie looked up at him in silence for a moment. Gus had never before spoken of his years as a slave.

"I still feel like I should go after her," she confessed. "I know I don't have any chance of saving her but I still feel that way. I can't simply sit here and do nothing!"

"You won't be doing nothing, Miss." Gus pointed at Riler. "You'll be healin' him up quick as can be. He'll go get her. He'll bring her back. I know it right down to the marrow in my bones."

"Why would he do that?" she asked, her voice reedy, her tone distraught.

Gus smiled. "You know why. There are some men who just will not stand by and let bad things happen to people. Reason I'm out here and not still in the South is on account of a man who bought me from a very bad man. It was the only way, back then and in that place, to save me, and he paid a lot more than I was worth. Lobo is the same kind of man. And he'll be on his feet before you know it. I mean, look at him, Miss Julie. He's all bone and sinew and grit and his skin is tough as whang leather. But you know what the strongest part of that man is? His heart."

"How do you know so much about him?"

"I can tell." Gus nodded, looking smug. "Yessum, I can tell."

Julie sighed and got up, telling Ana to go fetch the cloth hanging on the clothesline. It was time to dress Lobo Riler's wounds.

"I hope you're right," she told Gus. "I hope it won't be too late."

Chapter 13

Kelleren kept his crew moving long after nightfall, heading east on The Overland Trail in the direction of the Laramie River, and they put a good ten miles behind them before he told Sangre to pull the lead wagon into a small grove of cottonwoods and stop there. The other wagon and the riders followed. Kelleren grunted with pain as he climbed down out of the wagon box with only one good arm. The quarter-moon had risen in the east, shyly hiding behind clouds scudding in a southeasterly direction. With the sun long gone he could feel the bite of winter in his bones. Winter was always reluctant to loosen its hold on the mountains and high plains this time of year.

Sangre reminded him that the mules had not been fed and needed water, and Kelleren grimaced. He knew good and well what the mules needed. The plan had been that the knobheads would be tended to in Wild Horses around sunset, when it was more certain that they would be staying the night in town. So much for well-laid plans. He was in a generally sour mood all the way around, having expected to be in a nice warm bed with a nice warm whore. Instead he was standing wind-whipped, with bunched shoulders, in a grove of cottonwoods whose bare limbs were clattering overhead, cold and hungry and uncomfortable as hell.

"Feed 'em, but keep 'em in the traces. And 'fore you go tellin' me you could walk 'em down to the river, which I know as well as you do is a stone's throw north of us, I ain't going to risk losing one or more of them animals, not with three hundred dollars' worth of hides in these wagons. Get Chaytan to help you with the feed bags and to haul the water up. Make sure the water casks are filled when that's done, too. We won't find water this close again until we reach the Laramie River, and that's a long day and half of another up the trail."

Kelleren walked towards the second wagon. Everyone who had been mounted was out of the saddle now, most of them gathered round McNally, who was lying on the ground groaning in pain.

"You're a damn fool aren't you?" rasped Kelleren, without an ounce of sympathy for the skinner. "Did I *tell* you to go out and get that mountain man's scalp? Did I? And did you not notice that ol' trader comin' out of his post? You're damn lucky he was an old man. In his younger days Seth Topper was a good shot. When I…." He stopped abruptly, head swiveling, as he heard the crackle of dead limbs underfoot out in the blackness that gathered under the trees. A heartbeat later Texas Jack came into view with an armful of dead wood. "What are you aimin' to do with that?" asked Kelleren.

"Make a fire. It's colder than a witch's tit tonight, boss."

'There'll be no goddamn fire tonight, not until someone scouts our backtrail and makes certain we ain't been followed."

The hide hunters exchanged glances or shrugs.

"Who would be following us, anyhow?" asked Jonah Johnson.

"Who would be followin' us," mocked Kelleren. "Maybe that Indian boy. Must've been Topper's son the way he was carrying on. And does anyone here know for sure and certain that Lobo Riler is dead?"

There was a moment of silence. It was clear to Kelleren that most if not all of his men had assumed that the mountain man had died in the street.

Finally, Jim Early, who was still sitting in the box of the second wagon, said, "I shot him. And I know I killed him. I don't miss, 'specially at that range. Riler is dead. I'd bet my rifle on it."

"You go right ahead and do that. But I ain't gonna bet my life on it."

Early glared at him, then began to climb down off the wagon, bringing his rifle with him. "He didn't get up and keep fighting did he? And he would have if he could have. Seen enough of him to know that much be true. But it's fine, I'll ride back a ways." He snugged his long gun into its saddle sheath and swung astride the hull of a horse borrowed without asking and looked at Kelleren. "Don't go and shoot me when I ride back in," he cautioned.

"I just might," said Kelleren sullenly. "I don't much care for the way you talked to me just then."

Early shrugged bony shoulders to demonstrate his indifference, whipped his horse around and disappeared into the gloom of night.

Texas Jack had been staring at Rose, whose hands had been tied behind her back by Morris at some point during the ride. She sat huddled and naked on the ground where Morris had dropped her, her knees pulled up to her chin, shivering uncontrollably, avoiding eye contact with the men, a look of pure misery on her dirt-smeared, blood-caked face.

"What about her?" asked the former cowboy.

Morris had unsaddled the horse he had been riding and was down on one knee, pulling hardtack and some jerky out of a pouch and wolfing the food down. He looked up at Texas Jack, glaring. "She's mine," he mumbled, mouth full.

"The hell you say," barked Kelleren. "You're the reason we're here now, cold and hungry and some of us shot up. You don't get a reward for that. No, she belongs to the crew." He looked at the other men, a fierce glower on his rugged features. "If you have to knock her around a little to get what you want, that's fine. But I want her alive, and not marked up much more than she is." He turned his gaze on Sangre. "You bandage up her head, amigo."

The Mexican teamster nodded.

"We're keeping her?" asked Jonah Johnson, hopefully. For the first time since he'd been shot he wasn't feeling sorry for himself.

"For a spell. But after we sell these hides at Laramie we're heading south. We'll have ourselves another hunt, get another load, and go on down to the South Fork of the Platte. We can sell that load to Frenchy DuBois at his tradin' post. And I owe Frenchy a debt. She'll be my payment."

"What do you owe Frenchy for?" asked Jonah.

"Well, one day I'd imbibed a little too much of that snakehead poison Frenchy passes off as whiskey. I shot his mule. That was a mistake. I killed one of his whores. You know him, he likes to keep a couple of whores around for his customers, and himself. Well I killed one of 'em. Held her face down against the cornhusk mattress a little too long. She'd been cursing up a storm and callin' me all kinds of names. May be that she didn't think I knew what she was saying. But I knew, and didn't take it kindly — that, nor giving me trouble in getting what I'd paid Frenchy for. That was a couple years back, before you joined up with this company of fine, upstandin' gentlemen." Someone chuckled. "But he won't have forgotten. He usually just has squaws. The braves what get a taste for his rotgut would sometimes trade one of their squaws for a bottle, y'know. He'll be happy as all get out when he sees this one's yellow hair. What's left of it."

"Aw it'll grow back, Boss," said Texas Jack. "Probably won't even see the scars...too much."

"So you are all welcome to her," said Kelleren, "seeing as how Morris here saw fit to go fetch her instead of throwing in with us when we were in a fight. But I better not see anything on her but maybe some bruises when we get to the South Fork."

Rose sat there, trembling, and not entirely because of the night chill. She assumed Eldon Caulfield was dead, and on her account, and she was sorry about that. But what made her heart hurt was the glimpse she'd caught of Lobo Riler, face down in the street while Morris had dragged her across to the hide hunter wagons. Just thinking about it made her eyes glisten with tears. She wondered who else was dead because she hadn't listened to Julie and pretended to be sick when the four hide hunters came to the brothel. Thinking back to that fateful

     JASON MANNING

moment when she had appeared at the top of the stairs and announced her willingness to do her part in seeing to the needs of the men in the downstairs hallway with Julie, she had spent much of the day, while being transported belly down across a horse's withers, asking herself why she had done such a thing. The expression on Julie Regret's face as she looked up at her in that moment was a vision she knew she would never forget.

So why? Why had she done such a stupid thing? An act that had cost others their lives? She had never been one for introspection but this time was different. It wasn't hard to figure out. She had opened up to Lobo Riler like she never had to another man, made herself vulnerable to being hurt — and he had hurt her. Rejected her. Had left her feeling like a fool. A worthless fool. *And I guess that's what you are,* she told herself. Who else would do all that she had done in a desperate need to be loved? How stupid was it to be a shameless whore and expect the love of a man instead of his lust? This turned her morose thoughts to her father. The father who had always resented her for not being the son he had so desperately desired. She had been worthless the moment she was born. "You were right all along, "she whispered, talking to her father, then shook her head and wiped at the tears brimming over in her eyes.

'What did you say, girly?" asked Kelleren, leaning as he loomed over her. "You're not complainin' about your situation now are you? I mean, look around you. All these men who got a hankerin' for you." He chuckled, then grabbed her by the arm and yanked her roughly to her feet. "I 'member seein' you come running out of the whorehouse when we rolled into Wild Horses, with that golden hair in the mornin' sun, that pale skin." He brushed the back of his hand across her cheek. "Knew right then I was going to have you and looks like tonight's the night. What do you think about that?"

Rose looked up at him and smiled. "It's been my experience that the men who talk a lot often have trouble getting it up. But don't worry. I can help with that."

Kelleren blinked in surprise, stared at her a moment, then threw back his head and laughed heartily, braying like a mule.

"You've got grit, I'll give you that. But not going to fight me? I'm a little disappointed. Maybe I can change your mind. I like a whore with spirit." And with an ugly grin that chilled Rose, he tightened his grip on her arm and with long strides headed deeper into the night shadow gathered under the cottonwoods, dragging her along.

* * *

Rose Waldron woke the next morning cringing away from a man's touch. She sat up, wincing, and pulled her legs up and hugged them to her chest, looking wide-eyed at the swarthy visage of the one called Sangre. He held out his hand, palm towards her, and his tone was meant to be reassuring.

"*No te preocupes, niña. No te lastimaré.*" Brows furrowing, he thought a moment, then said, "I do not hurt you." And with that he offered her a canteen.

Rose realized then that someone had covered her with a blanket. She had a feeling it was the Mexican who had done it. At some point in the living nightmare of last night she had crawled under the lead wagon, curled up in a fetal ball, and fell into an exhausted sleep.

She drank from the canteen, quenching a raging thirst. Then she reached up to touch her head, realizing there was a makeshift dressing wrapped around it. Surprised, she looked at Sangre and he nodded. "Thank you," she murmured, and looked around the hide hunter's camp. There was a lot of activity — men saddling horses, others tying up their bedrolls, a couple huddling round a small fire trying to thaw the cold in their bones. Buckskin-clad Jim Early flashed a yellow, lecherous grin at her. Texas Jack glanced briefly at her when she sat up, and smiled faintly, looking ashamed of himself. She looked around for Kelleren and saw him standing a short distance away, up near the first wagon's mule team, wrapping a makeshift dressing round his upper arm, and she was relieved that he wasn't paying her any attention.

"*Aquí.* Come *esto.*"

She looked at the corn dodger Sangre was holding out to her, then took it and tried to bite into it. It was just about as hard as a rock. She

 JASON MANNING

poured some water from the canteen onto it, and when the Mexican teamster reached for the canteen she hugged it against her belly and then tried the dodger again. This time she could tear off a mouthful, giving Sangre a sidelong glance. He was watching her, his expression inscrutable.

"Thank you," she said, with her mouth full. "*Gracias.*"

He held out a hand and after she took another swig from the canteen she handed it to him. He made to rise then but she latched onto his wrist and pulled and he settled back down on his heels, as he had been before. Throwing a furtive look around, she whispered. "Will you help me? Please?

Sangre understood — she could tell by the look on his face. He shook his head. "*No. Lo siento por lo que hacen. Pero no moriré por ti.*"

Rose nodded. She understood the first word, and didn't need to understand the rest. "It's okay. I wouldn't want anyone else to die on my account." She hadn't had her hopes up and finished eating, thinking about what the men had done to her the night before. It had been a humiliating ordeal. *But you survived it, didn't you*, she told herself, trying to bolster her tattered self-respect. *You can survive anything, can't you.*

Sangre nodded and with the faintest of smiles on his ordinarily cruel mouth he rose and walked away.

She thought about Eldon Caulfield — the last time she had seen him, remembering how she had known then that he was going to die, and now she began to weep, silently, not wishing to draw attention to herself. It was one more thing to feel guilty about. Caulfield had died because she had agreed to marry him. There was no getting around that. And Julie Regret had been right — she hadn't loved him. She had only promised to do so because she had been so upset after Lobo Riler had rejected her. She didn't blame the mountain man for doing that. Who could blame him? *You're just a dirty little whore*, she told herself. *Why would any man want you for anything else besides what these men want you for?*

So lost was she in morose thoughts that she wasn't aware that Kelleren had walked up to her until she realized there were booted feet right in front of her. He wasn't leering at her this time but rather seemed to be studying her. Suddenly it mattered to her that he didn't think she was defeated and broken, so she got to her feet, holding the blanket around her slender, still shivering form, her chin lifted defiantly, even while her eyes glistened with tears.

Kelleren nodded curtly. "You can feel sorry for yourself all day long, girl, but it won't help. You know that. We make choices, we pay the price for 'em. That's life and ain't it grand." There was an undercurrent of bitter irony in his tone. "Oh, and by the way, Early came back. No one chasin' us. No one comin' to save you." He chuckled. "Looks like you belong to us. For now anyway. C'mon. You ride in the wagon with me and the Mex."

CHAPTER 14

When Lobo Riler regained consciousness the first thing he felt was something moist and cool on his forehead. Then it was gone, and all he felt after that was a gnawing and relentless pain that consumed the rest of his body. He groaned. His eyes fluttered open. His vision was blurred. He blinked several times and slowly the world came into focus. Julie Regret was looming over him, her eyes wide and filled with both relief and concern.

"Mr. Riler," she said. "Thank the Lord!"

He opened his mouth to respond, but all that came out was a hoarse croak. He felt her hand under his head, lifting it up a bit, and then felt the rim of a cup against his bottom lip and he sipped the water the cup contained, then began gulping it down and choked on it, coughing, and every time he coughed the pain that inhabited his body exploded into excruciating agony.

"I'm so sorry!" gasped Julie, distraught. "So sorry. I should have known better."

Riler licked his lips and tried again to speak. "Why?" he whispered.

"A long time ago, when I was young, I worked in a hospital in New Orleans. I was a nurse, though I had no proper schooling. I learned as I went along. And I should have known better than to try to make a man in your condition drink."

"What condition...am I in?" he asked.

"Well, you were shot. You remember, I assume?"

Riler nodded. He lifted a hand, touched the tight dressing round his midsection. "Not something you'd forget," he wheezed.

"I suppose it wasn't the first time."

Riler remembered the sensation of being shot all too vividly. It felt like a burning nail had been driven right through him. The impact had knocked him off his feet. Then the relentless, breathtaking pain. He remembered lying face down in the street, and the slightest movement just made that pain even more breathtaking. And then the world had slowly faded into a blood-red mist, followed by black oblivion.

He shook his head. "At least you're okay."

Julie sighed and nodded. "Yes, thanks to you. But others … were not so lucky, I'm sorry to say."

"Who?"

"Eldon Caulfield is dead. So is Seth Topper."

Riler nodded. "Dohasan. Seth's boy…"

"He's alive. He killed one of the hide hunters. Then he…."

"Then he what?"

Julie sighed again. "Then he stole an Overland horse and rode out after the rest."

"Damn it," hissed Riler, and tried to sit up. The agony that shot through him knocked the wind out of him and he fell back, panting. "Damn it," he muttered again. He had to catch his breath before asking, "How long ago?"

"Yesterday morning. The fight took place two days ago. The hide hunters moved out right after."

"How many?"

"Eight. The Heller brothers, they both died. You killed one of them. Mr. Caulfield shot the other. Then the one Dohasan killed…"

Riler touched the dressing again. "It went through me, didn't it?

You patched me up?"

She nodded. "No doctor here in Wild Horses. So I figured it was better for me to do it than anyone else. Stopped the bleeding with gunpowder, cleaned the entry and exit wounds with water and whiskey. Boiled the cloth before dressing it. And then all I could do for you was pray."

"Thank you." Riler was silent a moment, thinking about Topper, all the good times they had shared way back when, and about Topper's boy, wondering if he was still alive. He lifted his head slightly and looked around.

"You're in my room," said Julie. Then she noticed the scratching on the door and smiled and crossed the room and opened the door to let the wolfdog in. "He's been guarding you," she murmured, as the big black and gray beast went to the bed and sniffed Riler, then lay its head down next to the mountain man's hand. "Lay down in front of that door and hasn't budged since. Quite an amazing friend you have there, Mr. Riler. He came out of nowhere during the fight, lay down on top of you after you fell. I was surprised when he let me and Gus move you."

"Reckon he knew you were trying to help me," said Riler, laying his hand on the wolfdog's head.

"I suppose. I am the only person he will let through the door. Gus tried. So did the girls."

"Your girls are unharmed?"

Julie was silent a moment, nearly overwhelmed by strong emotions. Tears glistened in her eyes. Riler could see the agony in her expression — a different kind of agony than the one in which he languished, but just as severe it seemed.

"What?" he rasped. "What's wrong?"

Julie drew a long, ragged breath. "Well, you see, the hide hunters ... they took Rose."

This time Riler managed to sit up, though it cost him dearly. Alarmed by how pale he suddenly became, Julie hurried back to the bed and put hands on his shoulders and tried to push him, gingerly, back down.

"Don't be a fool, Mr. Riler! You'll start bleeding again. And if you lose much more blood you'll die! You lost at least a quart of blood, probably more. That's why you passed out in the street. "It will take a day or two for your body to produce about a pint of blood. So you need to rest at least a week and preferably two. If you don't, and you start bleeding again, then there will be no saving you."

As much as he wanted to get on his feet, Riler had to accept the truth of what she said, and the fact that if he died he would be of no help to Dohasan … or Rose. If they weren't beyond help already. In a perfect anguish, both physical and emotional, he relented and let her push him back down onto his back.

"No one went after her?"

"I should have," said Julie, and a single tear escaped down her cheek. She wiped it away.

Riler shook his head. "No. Tell me, what started the trouble?"

Julie sank into the chair in which she had spent most of the last two days, rubbed her bloodshot eyes — she hadn't slept a wink since the fight — and pinched the bridge of her nose as she grimly reviewed the sequence of events that had led to the trouble, looking down at her hands, clasped tightly in her lap.

"I was about to say Mr. Caulfield started it. But the truth is, Rose did. She told me Mr. Caulfield had proposed to her and she accepted, and that they were going off to San Francisco. Mr. Caulfield had gone off to arrange transportation for them when four of the hide hunters showed up at the house. I told Rose to stay in her room, that I would tell the hide hunters that she was very sick and highly contagious. Instead, she came out of her room and … flaunted herself in front of them." Julie shook her head and sighed "I cannot even begin to imagine why she did such a thing. Can you? She didn't love Eldon Caulfield. Honestly, I'm not sure that girl could love anyone. But then Mr. Caulfield comes back and I try to stop him from going into the Regret, but he knows the hide hunters are inside and he barges in, gun drawn. He kills Emmett Heller who was waiting in my parlor, then charges upstairs and — well, after that I'm not sure what happened. But the end result is that he is dead, and Rose has been hauled off. But not after

                    JASON MANNING

that one called Morris all but scalped her, saying he wanted a memento. He took more than just a lock of her hair, I can tell you." She looked up at Riler then, and the expression on his face alarmed her, and she got to her feet and went to the bed. "Is something wrong?"

Riler hardly heard the question. He was lost in thought — and in regrets and self-recrimination — as he realized he knew the answer to Julie's question. He *did* know why Rose had accepted Caulfield's offer. It was because he had revealed to her how much he needed her, wanted her, in ways that went beyond physical release, and in so doing had given her hope, the possibility that she could have a life different from the one she led, the one she convincingly pretended was the only life she ever wanted. But the memory of Quahneah had burdened him with guilt and he had taken back the offer as soon as it was made. He had offered her hope and then snatched it away.

"Mr. Riler?"

He looked up at Julie Regret, his eyes bleak. He wanted to tell her that the gunfight which had resulted in the deaths of Seth Topper and Eldon Caulfield and three hide hunters had not been Rose Waldron's doing. It was *his* doing. But something, some instinct, warned him not to, that telling Julie what had happened between him and Rose would lead to more hurt.

"I'm fine," he said flatly.

She didn't believe him. "I have a bottle of laudanum, about half full. I'll get you some in the event that the pain becomes too much."

Riler shook his head adamantly. "No, none of that." He wanted the pain. He wanted to suffer through it. Not only would it give him a more accurate idea of when he could get up and move around but he figured that Rose Waldron was suffering every minute of the day and night and he was determined to do the same.

Julie looked at him for a moment in silence. She sensed that there was something he wasn't telling her, and assumed it had to do with his physical condition and discomfort. "Well," she murmurs, "I'm going to go down to the kitchen and start some supper. I'll bring you a plate, should you feel like eating."

He nodded, and she went to the door and opened it – and gasped.

Gus Freeman stood there, a fist raised. He had been about to knock.

"Sorry, Miss Julie, if I startled you," he said. "I come to see how Lobo's doing."

Julie stepped aside and gestured at the bedridden mountain man. "He just regained consciousness. I would say he's doing better than I expected he would be. I'm going down to cook supper. You are welcome to stay and eat." She smiled politely and eased past him and walked down the hall towards the stairs.

Gus stepped across the threshold and then stopped dead in his tracks as the wolfdog growled.

"Easy," said Riler, to the wolfdog. "Stay with me." He looked up at Gus. "Good to see you."

Gus grinned. "Good to see you still above snakes, Lobo. Wish I could've done more during the dust-up. But with my eyes being the way they are I'd have likely shot you than one of those hide hunters. I'm real sorry about Ol' Seth Topper. I know he was a friend of yours. I buried him myself, out a ways, near Smoking Woman. Hope that suits you, seeing as how we ain't got a graveyard here."

Riler grimaced, silent a moment as he thought about his old friend's lifeless body six feet under. Gus remained in the doorway, still uncertain about the wolfdog that was watching him. "I spoke over his grave. 'Let not your hearts be troubled. Believe in God; believe also in me. In my Father's house are many rooms. If it were not so, would I have told you that I go to prepare a place for you? And if I go and prepare a place for you, I will come again and will take you to myself, that where I am you may be also. And you know the way to where I am going.' John, Chapter Fourteen."

Riler managed to paste a smile back on his face. He knew that Gus Freeman couldn't read, but he had a good memory, as he had remembered a good deal of the Bible just from listening to others quoting scripture. "Thanks for doing that, Gus."

The blacksmith nodded. "I just wish I'd been able to stop Dohasan from lightin' out after them hide hunters. You reckon he's still alive?"

"I have no idea," was Riler's bleak reply. "But I'll find out."

"You aimin' to go after those men when you're able, do you?"

"Damn right."

"On account they killed your friend?"

"That and other reasons."

"I done told Mrs. Regret that you would. That nothin' could stop you." He paused, looking down at his boots. "And I would be much obliged if you let me go with you when you do. I know I can't shoot worth a lick. I know I can't read sign like you do. Even so, I would be obliged."

Riler looked at him a moment, nodding slowly. He thought he understood the blacksmith's motivation, remembering the day when he had been a greenhorn among the free trappers, many of whom had been veterans of the old Rocky Mountain Fur Company, when he had been trying to learn the trade and eager to prove himself to the likes of Seth Topper and Jedediah Smith and Jim Bridger.

"You'll most likely get killed, you know," he said. "I most likely will, too."

"I ain't afraid of dyin'," Gus smiled pensively. "For one thing, I may get to see Smoking Woman again. See, I reckon there's just one Heaven, be you red, white or black, and that the Great Spirit and Jehovah are one in the same."

Riler thought about Quahneah then, and wondered if he would see her again. But he didn't have the faith of Gus Freeman, and just sighed, gave a little shake of the head.

"Please, Lobo, I won't be a burden."

Riler nodded. "Okay."

Gus was grinning again, this time ear to ear. "Thank you! Thank you so much! You won't regret it."

"Well, if I do, what's one more regret?"

"So, you reckon a couple of weeks?"

"Hell no," growled Riler. "What's today?"

"It's Wednesday."

"Come back and be ready to ride on Monday."

"Yes, sir, Mr. Lobo! Yes, sir!"

* * *

When Julie Regret returned to her room an hour after bringing Riler some supper, she was pleasantly surprised to see that the bowl she had filled with stew was empty and the slice of bread that had accompanied the stew was gone, too.

"Good for you, Mr. Riler! You'll regain your strength more quickly if you can eat."

"I'm sure not going to pass up a chance for food cooked by someone other than me."

She smiled, checking the dressing around his midsection. "I reckon I'll need to change this in the morning."

"I want to thank you for all you've done."

"No need to thank me. It will be reward enough to see you up and around in a couple of weeks."

"I won't be here in a couple of weeks. I'll be ridin' out Monday."

Julie opened her mouth to protest, then shut it without a word said. She realized how futile it would be to argue with this man. So she just nodded and gathered up the bowl. At the door she paused and turned just her head. "Will you be coming back this way, Mr. Riler?"

"I will. But you won't see those hide hunters in Wild Horses again. Not a single damn one of them."

 JASON MANNING

CHAPTER 15

When the hide-laden lead wagon crested a rise and Rose could see the valley of the Laramie River stretched about as far as the eye could see before her, she was relieved. The fort was a large one, and to the south of it along the river was a sizeable town of tents and makeshift structures where traders, gamblers, and peddlers of cheap whiskey and cheaper whores were engaged in a brisk business with soldier and settler alike. She calculated that there were at least a couple of hundred people down there, mostly men, and she entertained the hope that something might happen that would result in her rescue from Kelleren and his gang.

She sat wedged between Kelleren and Sangre. She still had the blanket that the latter had given her, draped over her shoulders. At least they were no longer keeping her hands tied behind her back. This was the fourth day since their departure from Wild Horses, and every night had been an ordeal for her. She had never put up a fight but even so some of the hide hunters had treated her roughly. Morris in particular had been hard on her. She figured that it was Kelleren's warning to the other men not to damage her too badly that was the only explanation for the fact that she wasn't bruised and broken beyond recognition. Even so she ached from head to toe, and her private parts had started hurting the day before. She feared she might have some kind of infection. She was filthy, too, as they had not seen a water source since that first night. The Laramie River looked very inviting, and she wished she could just lay in it, let it carry her away. Unfortunately, while wide, the river was shallow and languid and it would not carry her swiftly enough to escape this living hell in which she found herself.

She had seen Fort Laramie before. The wagon train with which she and her folks traveled had passed this way. Thanks to her father she knew a lot about the fort. William Waldron was a well-read man and he liked to show off how much he knew about things whenever the opportunity arose, so she had heard all there was to hear about the garrison.

Initially a trading post had been built on the site, here in the heart of Cheyenne and Arapaho hunting grounds. It wasn't a fort but it was called one anyway — Fort William. Belong long, more and more westward-bound wagon trains were stopping here, not so much for the amenities provided by the trading post, which Rose imagined had been few and far between, but because of the river. It was a good place to rest a day or two, to water stock, to bathe and wash clothes.

A real fort — an adobe one — was eventually built, on a long low bluff on the eastern side of the river. It was christened Fort John but had come to be known as Fort Laramie. Some years later the United States government realized the value of the location and bought the place. More and more settlers were moving west, and more and more trouble with the Indians occurred as a result. Congress had appropriated funds for the establishment of forts along the Oregon Trail and a regiment of mounted riflemen to occupy them. Fort Laramie was the second of these outposts.

Oddly enough, while a perimeter stockade was planned, it never came to fruition. Laramie was a fort without walls. But it grew in a sprawl of buildings that covered the bluff. The size of its garrison now, coupled with the population of the adjacent tent town, made it unlikely

     JASON MANNING

that a single tribe could bring a sufficient number of braves together to mount a successful attack. According to her father, the animosity that existed between the various Plains tribes was generations old and not easily set aside, so that the level of cooperation required to produce an effective resistance to the encroachment of the white man was impossible to achieve. So far, at least.

Kelleren had been in a grim mood these past two days. He insisted that they were being followed, even though Early and even the Indian, Chaytan, could not find any evidence of it. And his wound was hurting him, as it had begun to fester. He was as relieved as Rose to see Fort Laramie.

"It's a shame I have to give you over to ol' Frenchy down on the South Fork. Why I bet there's two hunnerd men down there, and maybe twenty, thirty whores and none of them as easy on the eyes as you. I could set you up in a tent and at a dollar a poke would make as much off you in a month as we're likely see for this entire load of buffalo hide."

"What a shame," said Rose, sardonically.

Kelleren's toothy grin faded. He gripped her arm and squeezed it hard enough to make her wince and gasp.

"You got a smart mouth on you, girl. Better not take that tone with Frenchy. He'll cut your tongue out. Only words that better come out of that mouth of yours are please, thank you, and yes sir." He let go of her arm and surveyed the outpost of civilization that stretched for a good half mile along the east bank of the river. "When we get over there you best just keep your mouth shut and not say a one damned word. You hear? Ain't nobody there going to help you. Especially not the soldiers. They're the worst of the lot."

"*Fue por los soldados que dijiste que no querías venir aquí,*" commented Sangre. "*Por qué querías que ese comerciante vuelva a Wild Horses para comprar las pieles. ¿No es así?*"

"Yeah that's right," rasped Kelleren, perturbed. "I didn't want to come here. But now we don't have a choice, do we? Now we have to try to sell the hides. With any luck we can get that done nice and quick and the soldiers won't pay us no mind, and then we head south."

When they reached the river the mules waded in hock deep and began to drink. Sangre pulled a bullwhip out of its stock and was about to get them moving again when Kelleren stopped him. "Let 'em drink. We may have to get out of here fast." He got down out of the box, gingerly and without using his right arm. Then he reached up with his left hand and latched onto Rose and pulled her out of the box and let go so that she sprawled in the muddy shallows with a great splash.

Kelleren cut loose with a belly laugh as she came up spluttering. The water-logged blanket came off her shoulders and the river's current began to carry it away. She scrambled after it and caught it but at the same time stubbed her toes on a stone embedded in the river sand and fell face-first into the water. When she tried to get up again, Kelleren reached down and yanked the blanket out of her grasp, then put a booted foot on her shoulder and pushed her down into the water, submerging her. Her arms flailed above the surface and then she latched onto his leg. He grinned as he felt her writhing and flopping underfoot. Sangre leaned over and looked down from the wagon, growing concern on his face as he saw Rose's grip on Kelleren's leg loosen, and then her arms fell away to either side and began to sink. Also concerned all of a sudden, Kelleren reached under the surface and pulled her up. Rose came up spluttering and laughing breathlessly, much to the astonishment of all the hide hunters present.

"You're not going to murder me," she said, with a degree of insolence mingled with confidence. "You need me. Your stinking men need me. You want me alive more than I care if I stay alive." She wrenched her arm free, a defiant look on her face.

Taken aback, Kelleren angrily backhanded her. The blow knocked her sideways. She fell into the wagon wheel and grabbed hold of it, bringing a hand up to her face. Her lip was split and bleeding. Texas Jack spurred his horse forward until he was between Kelleren and the girl. He looked gravely down at the former and said, in a quiet drawl, "What the hell are you doing, Boss? You told us not to mark her. What are you doing?"

Kelleren looked up at the former cowboy, then around at the faces of the other hide hunters. He took a long deep breath and nodded.

     JASON MANNING

"Let's get moving," he growled, then turned his bleak gaze on Texas Jack. "Get out of my way." Texas Jack urged his horse forward and Kelleren looked coldly at Rose. "Get up in the wagon."

Rose climbed up into the bench and sat down next to Sangre. Kelleren threw the water-laden blanket at her, then clambered up onto the bench, after her.

"Put that on," he said. "Don't need to be drawin' too much attention to ourselves." He nodded at Sangre, who stirred up the mules and the wagon began to roll.

Once they had crossed the wide but shallow Laramie, Kelleren directed Sangre to drive the wagon deep into the middle of the tent town. Huddled in the robe that clung heavy and damp to her slender body, Rose gazed wide-eyed at all the people. There was no rhyme or reason to the placement of the makeshift shanties and tents, which formed a byzantine puzzle through which Sangre somehow managed to maneuver the wagon, until Kelleren hollered at him to stop alongside a large blood-red tent. Two men emerged from the deep shadow of the tent's interior. The older one was short, stocky, with a crop of curly carrot-colored hair on his head and a ruddy, square-jawed face. The other man was younger, thin as a fence post, with his dusty black frock coat pushed back so that he could keep a bony-fingered hand resting on the butt of a holstered pistol.

"Well as I live and breathe," said the older man. "It was Herodotus who said 'He who the gods love dies young' and that must be why we're both still alive." Grinning, he stepped up to the wagon and extended a hand up. "If you've come to sell those hides then you've come to the right place. I'm offering a dollar a hide today. If you're interested, come on into the tent and we'll have a drink."

Kelleren grinned and nodded. He took the hand and shook it enthusiastically. "Clapton, you son-of-a-bitch, it's good to see you. But I know you'll get at least three dollar a hide from a tannery, so we'll have to do some haggling. I'll take a dollar and a half and not a penny less."

Clapton chuckled and glance past Kelleren at Rose. "And who might this be?"

"Just a whore," said Kelleren, clambering down off the wagon.

"Is she hurt?"

Kelleren looked up at Rose and realized it was the dirty cloth around the woman's head that had prompted Clapton's question.

"Nah. Fell down and cut her head, but she'll be fine."

Clapton studied Rose a moment longer, brows furrowed, but since Rose didn't say anything and looked away, he lost interest. "Fair enough. Have to be careful in a place like this. A sickness can spread like wildfire in this kind of environment, this many people packed together in one spot."

"If she had a sickness she wouldn't be travelin' with me," said Kelleren.

Clapton nodded and turned towards the tent from which he had come, with a follow-me gesture.

Kelleren motioned for Texas Jack and the ex-cowboy urged his horse forward.

"Everybody stays with the wagons," said Kelleren. "Don't let nobody wander off. If you see even one soldier, you come and tell me. Got that?"

Texas Jack nodded and turned his horse around and walked it back to the others on horseback, who were grouped between the wagons. On the way he passed Morris, who had dismounted and now approached Kelleren.

"Boss, while we waitin' I'm of a mind to have me a little fun with the whore."

Kelleren snorted derisively. "We're trying to get in here and sell these hides and then get out without drawing attention to ourselves. A black man raping a white girl would draw plenty of attention, I reckon. You keep your hands off her or I'll do what I've had a hankerin' to do since we left Wild Horses."

Morris didn't fail to notice that Kelleren's hand was resting on the butt of his pistol. He nodded and sullenly turned away, climbing back up into the box of the second wagon.

Kelleren looked over at Sangre. "Keep an eye on the whore. She doesn't get down off that wagon." Then he turned and followed the trader into his tent.

 JASON MANNING

Sangre tied up the mule team's leathers and glanced at Rose. "*Usted corre, tendré que dispararle,*" he said, and to be certain that she understood, he struggled to put the warning into English. "You try run I shoot."

He jumped down off the wagon and began checking the mules and the hitch. Rose took a long look around at the bustling tent town. There were a lot of people about, and it was possible that some of them would be inclined to help her — or try to anyway. But she doubted that Kelleren or his men would give her up without a fight. So if she called out for help, men would probably die on her account. And enough men had already done that. With a sigh she stretched out on the wagon bench. Wearing a wool blanket that had been soaked in the river on a briskly cool day wasn't pleasant, but it was better than being naked, and she started to doze off while listening to McNally complaining about the order to stay with the wagons. Someone had dug the buckshot out of his legs the first night out of Wild Horses, but couldn't get to one wedged against the bones in a knee, and now an infection had set in and McNally had come down with a fever and he was desperate to see a doctor. Texas Jack explained that McNally needed money to pay for a doctor and so he had to wait until a deal was struck between Kelleren and the trader for the load of hides. McNally was still complaining as she drifted off into an exhausted sleep.

She woke with a start, startled by the shouts of men, and sat up quickly.

Blue-coated soldiers had surrounded the two wagons, all of them on foot, all of them with guns drawn. Most of them were armed with carbines. One of them, though, whom she took to be an officer due to the epaulets on the shoulders of his tunic and the fact that he wore a wide-brimmed hat rather than forage cap, as the others wore, was carrying a pistol. She assumed he was an officer. Beyond the ring of soldiers, the denizens of the tent town had vanished. Not a single person aside from the soldiers and the hide hunters was visible.

Chapter 16

Rose turned her attention back to the officer. He was a tall, slender man who was looming over the shorter, stockier Kelleren, who had come out of the tent to stand with his back to Rose and the wagon. She could clearly see the officer's angular face, the sneering curl of thin lips beneath a bushy black mustache, eyes gleaming with triumph. She knew that Kelleren wanted to avoid any soldiers, and so she realized that this could be her chance — probably her one and only chance — to be rescued from the hide hunters.

"Better tell your men to drop their guns," the officer told Kelleren. "These soldiers have orders to shoot if there is any resistance." Then he raised his Colt Army revolver and pressed the end of the barrel against Kelleren's forehead, right above the bridge of his nose, and grinned. "But if you don't want to do that then by all means, don't. I'll be happy to put you down right here and now."

Rose couldn't see Kelleren's expression, but she heard the cold anger in his tone when he called out, "You boys drop your guns. Now, damn you!"

In the moment of silence broken only by the clatter of pistols and rifles being thrown to the ground, Rose saw her chance and cried, "Please, Sir! Help me!"

The officer looked up at her, startled.

"Please, my name is Rose Waldron and…"

Kelleren turned his head to look at her, and his eyes were as cold as muddy ice.

"Quiet!" snapped the officer, then turned his attention back to Kelleren — and grinned. "I was hoping you would be foolish enough to come back here, Kelleren. That's why I made sure our sentries knew to come inform me if any hide hunters rolled in. There have been a half-dozen crews pass through already since the river ice melted but I didn't give up hope. And here by God you are!"

"Now, now, Lieutenant Telford, no need for all this. I didn't just come here to sell my hides. I came to settle accounts with you."

Telford laughed. He stepped back, the barrel of his Colt parting company with Kelleren's head, but he kept the pistol aimed at the hide hunter's chest and tapped his shoulders with his free hand. "You see this? Two bars. I'm not a lieutenant anymore. I'm a captain, and I'm in command here at Fort Laramie. Now I didn't get that second bar by being a fool. I know for damn sure you never intended to 'settle accounts' with me. Tell me, how much did Clapton pay you for your load of hides? And don't lie to me, because all I have to do is go ask him and he'll tell me the truth because he doesn't want to get run out of here."

"Three hundred dollars," said Kelleren, glumly.

"Well let's see. Two years ago you came to me and said you wanted to hunt shaggies. You knew there was money to be made. You also knew that the army was encouraging the hunting of the buffalo. I sold you these wagons for sixty dollars apiece, and twelve mules at twenty-five dollars a head. You came back this time last year and sold a load of hides and paid me a hundred dollars. Told me you were heading back out to hunt again, and would bring me the rest. But, as I found out later, you sold those hides to a trader down at Crawford's Forge. That fellow is up here now and I've made sure no one down there will do business with you. After you give me that three hundred, you're still short twenty dollars."

Telford glanced at the other hide hunters who, save for Sangre, were bunched up around the saddle and pack horses tied up between that wagon and the second. Sangre stood at the head of the first wagon's mule team. Turning his attention back on Kelleren, Telford said, "By the looks on their faces, you never told them any of this, did you?"

Texas Jack was glaring at Kelleren. "Well at least now we know why you wanted to try sneakin' in and out of here," he drawled.

"Listen," said Kelleren. "I'll give you a hundred and fifty. But I need to pay these men for the work they've done. If they don't get paid I can't guarantee that they won't kick up some dust."

The captain laughed, gestured at the armed soldiers forming a ring around the two wagons. "I don't give a good goddamn. They can turn on you and I won't object. But if they cause any trouble they'll be gunned down or hanged. You see, I'm not just a captain, I'm the judge, jury and executioner around here." He held out a hand. "I'll thank you to hand over what you owe me. Count yourself lucky that I'm not confiscating the wagons and mule teams. Legally, they still belong to me. But I wouldn't want to put you out of business." Then he fastened his gaze on Rose. "And I'll take her, too, in lieu of the other twenty dollars you owe me." He stepped closer to the wagon. "Though she's in pretty poor shape, by the looks of it. What happened to you, girl?" He motioned to his head.

Rose was startled, but realized he meant the filthy makeshift bandaging around her head. She looked around for Morris, eyes narrowing, thinking perhaps she could get the black bastard who had cut her and nearly taken her ear in the process into trouble.

"She damn near got scalped," said Kelleren. "There's a man called Lobo. One of the last of the mountain men. Maybe the last, for all I know. He come down to Wild Horses, up on the Overland Trail, and went loco a few days back. Killed some of the folks who live there. Killed three of my men, too."

Rose stared at Kelleren, aghast. "That's not true!" she gasped.

      Jason Manning

The captain turned to Kelleren. "Did you kill this mountain man?"

Kelleren shook his head. "No. We lit out. Brought the woman with us to save her life. If we hadn't, that bastard would have killed her, too."

"He's lying!" cried Rose.

"Be quiet," snapped the captain. He took Kelleren's by the arm and led him ten paces away from the wagon. "Why do I have this feeling you're lying to me?"

"I ain't lying," replied Kelleren. "And you don't want that woman. She's nothing but trouble."

"Of course. She's a woman. Last one I had was a Paiute squaw. She was brought here a couple of summers ago by a mustanger. I won her in a poker game. I'm the best poker player north of the Cimarron, but he didn't know that. She was young and pretty but she was hell on wheels. She gave me some trouble. Now she's dead."

"Listen, I'm telling you this because that Lobo feller will most likely be coming after the girl. He's obsessed with her. And it will be feather in the cap of whoever brings to justice the man responsible for the massacre at Wild Horses."

The captain scanned the wagons, counting hide hunters. "You're scared of this man Lobo."

"I ain't scared of no man."

"You got seven men with you, and you're telling me you ran away from him?"

"That Lobo, he's a bushwhacker and backstabber. You know how them mountain men are. Worse than Injuns. You don't see him until he's killing you. We're hide hunters, Captain, not soldiers. We ain't getting paid to die."

The captain rubbed his chin, deep in thought for a moment. "What does this mountain man look like?"

"You can't miss him. He rides a tall buckskin horse and has a dog with him what looks like a wolf. Might be one, for all I know."

"You're coming with me, Kelleren. To my office. My orderly will write up a statement and you'll sign it, or put your mark on it."

"I can write my name," said Kelleren resentfully.

The captain laughed. "I'm not sure I believe you about this business at Wild Horses, or that you have that woman out of the goodness of your heart. But if what you say is true then you're right, it will be a feather in my cap if I deal with that mountain man. And since I'm the law here, I *can and will* deal with him. As for the truth of a matter, it just depends on who's left standing, doesn't it." He glanced at Rose, still huddled in the blanket on the bench of the first wagon. "Fetch her."

Kelleren grimaced. He didn't cotton to being ordered around like a lackey by anyone, least of all this man. But he fully understood his predicament. If he gave the captain any trouble at all he could end up in the Laramie brig. And as the captain had made a point of saying, he was the only law in these parts and it was possible he could die with a rope around his neck. For someone who represented the lawless, Telford was a lawless man. The wagons and mules had not been his to sell, being the property of the United States Army. How he had gotten away with that Kelleren didn't know and wasn't going to ask.

As for the lie about what had transpired in Wild Horses, he knew the captain was skeptical. He also knew it didn't matter. He had told a good story, the kind of tale that would resonate among people on the frontier, and often enough facts were not allowed to get in the way of a good story. A shootout was pretty ordinary business in these parts, but a massacre? Now that was a story, and the man responsible for bringing the perpetrator of the crime to justice would become famous, and there were many possible rewards that could accompany fame. Telford was would not be bothered by facts when he could claim to be the man responsible for killing the man responsible for the Massacre at Wild Horses.

Reaching the lead wagon Kelleren looked bleakly up at Rose and said, "Get down. You're staying here."

Rose looked past him at the captain. "Why is that?" she asked, clearly suspicious.

"Because I'm giving you to him as part of the payment of a debt. Or would you rather stay with us and get poked a half dozen times every night until we get to the South Fork?"

 Jason Manning

"You lied about what happened in town," she said. "I'll tell him the truth."

Kelleren chuckled bitterly. "Don't matter. *You* don't matter. Get that through your thick skull. You're only good for one thing."

Rose did not have to deliberate for more than a few seconds. Certain that whatever happened in the future could not be as bad as the last few days had been, she got down out of the wagon, holding the blanket closed round her neck. Kelleren took her by the arm and brought her to the captain.

Telford did a slow walk around her, smiling as he said, "You'll be staying with me for a time, girl. But first, let me get a look at you. Open up that blanket."

Rose turned pale, her eyes darting past the captain, at the ring of soldiers, those standing close enough to overhear looking at her now. But she lowered her eyes and opened the blanket, exposing her dirty, slender, naked body. She could feel their eyes on her.

The captain stepped closer, and leaned in to speak softly, his lips inches from her ear, and while he spoke he reached up to grope and fondle one of her breasts. "You listen well, and remember what I say here. The last woman who gave me trouble died an unpleasant death. You do as you're told, and you will stay alive. Understand?"

"Yes," whispered Rose, trembling, but through sheer force of will stood still and kept the blanket held open wide.

The captain groped her a moment longer, but she didn't move, and her expression remained stony. This seemed to displease Telford and he frowned at her, then abruptly turned and shouted, "Sergeant, take this woman to my orderly. Tell him to get her cleaned up and have the surgeon take a look at her."

A short, stocky soldier with three chevrons sewn to his sleeves came forward. He brought his knuckles to the brim of his forage cap in a salute, and said, "Yes, Sir, right away, Sir," while his eyes lingered on Rose's naked body.

The captain turned back to her. "Cover yourself. Go with this man. Do what you're told. That's what you'll do from now on, you hear? Do what you're told. Nothing more. Nothing less."

Rose wrapped the blanket around here, gave a small nod. The sergeant took her by the arm and led her away.

The captain turned his attention back to Kelleren. "Why are you still here? Take your crew and get moving."

It troubled Kelleren more than he thought it would to see Rose Waldron escorted away. But it bothered him even more to resort to begging, yet he saw no other option.

"I will," he said, "but at least let me keep enough of the money Clapton paid me so's I can pay my men. Then I can go on another hunt and be back in a month or six weeks and I'll pay you the rest of what I owe you then. You have my word."

The captain snorted derisively. "We've seen what your word is worth."

"I got no reason now to hide from you. I'll come back and we'll settle this debt once and for all."

Telford studied him for a moment, then shrugged. His mind was on the girl now. He glanced over at Kelleren's crew again, then counted out a hundred and fifty dollars in the ten-dollar legal tender bills that featured a red seal and a picture of Abraham Lincoln with which Clapton had bought the hides. Before he handed over the cash he held it up in front of Kelleren's face.

"You be sure to come back and settle this account once and for all," he said sternly. "If you don't, I'll hunt you down and hang you and your whole damned crew right along with you."

Kelleren nodded. He wanted to snatch the money he believed was rightfully his out of the captain's hand and then punch the man in the face for good measure. But odds were good he would be dead immediately after, so instead he stood there and held out his hand, palm up, like a beggar. When the captain placed the bills in his hand he turned quickly and walked with angry strides back to the wagons.

"Where they takin' the whore?" asked Morris.

"Shut the hell up," growled Kelleren, as he handed two bills to each man.

"But what we s'pose to do tonight, without her to poke?"

"Do what you were doing all winter. Now mount up. We're

 JASON MANNING

heading east. Going to get another load of hides."

"What about my leg?" whined McNally.

"You stay here. Get your leg tended. We'll be back in a month, maybe less." Kelleren looked at the other men. "What are you standing around for? Let's GO!"

CHAPTER 17

Fort Laramie looked to Rose more like a prosperous town rather than an army stronghold. It wasn't just the absence of a perimeter wall. It was also the wide thoroughfares and the sturdy, well-kept buildings. Some of them were quite imposing — like the one the sergeant informed her was Old Bedlam, the post headquarters. Old Bedlam not only had a long wide porch running its full length, but a balcony on the second floor that did likewise, accessible by staircases at either end of the structure. Its walls were framed brick and it sported two huge chimneys. It had been built, he informed her, in 1849, and was the first military structure on the site. That was back before the outpost was called Fort Laramie.

A bit further along was a rambling, one-story frame house with a wrap-around porch. This, the sergeant said, would be her new home — the residence of the commanding officer, Captain Telford. He grinned as he imparted this information to her. Once inside, he hustled her down a long wide hallway and into a room at the back that sported a clawfoot tub. The sergeant kicked the door shut and only then did he let go of her arm, only to snatch the blanket away from her. He looked her over, grinning, and then pointed at a cabinet with a built-in enamel sink and water pump.

"Clean yourself up. Use the soap and be thorough. Then I'll take you to the infirmary to see Doc Eldemann."

Rose looked at him. "You're going to stand there and watch," she murmured.

"Hell yes I'm going to watch," said the sergeant, chuckling. "You look like you've lived in a pig pen but I'll wager you're a right pretty gal under all that filth. Besides…" He pointed with his chin at the window above the tub. "You try to get away and the captain will have my scalp." He leaned forward and pitched his voice low, as though he was sharing a secret. "The captain isn't a fellow you want to anger, believe me."

Rose sighed. "I believe you." She had never seen a water pump inside a building before. She filled the basin two-thirds full, took up the brick of soap and sniffed it. This was not lard soap, but smelled of olive oil. She gingerly removed the filthy, bloodstained bandaging around her head.

"What in the blue blazes happened to you?" asked the sergeant, shocked.

"An admirer wanted a lock of my hair," said Rose bitterly.

"Well he took a lot more than a lock, I'd say." Rose nodded, gingerly touching her ear. She wondered what it looked like, then wondered if she really wanted to know. She touched her half-shorn scalp. "Yeah," she said, morosely. "He took a lot more."

Her hair was matted and snarled and dirty and she spent some time washing it. Then she gave herself a whore's bath, something she was very familiar with, as she had often washed herself in her room at the Regret in between customers. The act itself had her missing Ana and Molly, and particularly Julie Regret. The sergeant tossed her a towel to dry off with, and then pointed at the floor in front of the cabinet. There was quite a bit of water on the floor.

"Clean that up," he said.

Rose got down on hands and knees and dried the floor thoroughly.

The sergeant did a slow walk around her, and she knew he wasn't looking at the floor. She realized that there had been a time when she craved such attention, sought it with her words and actions, brazenly showing off her willowy body. She didn't crave it now, though and made a quick and thorough job of wiping up the water.

The sergeant helped her up and led her into an adjacent room. It was a bedroom, and Rose's heart lurched in her chest. But the sergeant just went to a large wooden trunk at the foot of the bed, opened it, pulled out a gray Army-issue woolen blanket and tossed it to her, telling her to wrap up in it. It barely covered her hips, but at this point she was grateful for anything, especially as sundown was approaching and the air was becoming decidedly colder.

She was taken across a very wide parade ground, with scattered trees around the perimeter, and to one of a row of single-story, white-washed adobe-and-clapboard buildings. She was led through a door above which hung a sign reading INFIRMARY, and inside she met the post surgeon, Dr. Eldemann.

The post surgeon was a slender, tall, white-haired man who appeared to be at least sixty years of age. He was sitting in a well-appointed office in the front of the building, complete with glass-front bookcases filled to overflowing with books and newspapers and cloth-bound journals. Thick carpets lay here and there on a clean but worn puncheon floor. Eldemann was bent over a roll-top desk when the sergeant brought Rose in and explained that he had delivered the woman on the orders of Telford.

Eldemann looked at Rose for a long moment without saying a word, his bushy gray brows knitted, an expression of disapproval on his deeply lined face. He gestured her to come closer to his chair, and when she was close enough he gently took her by the chin and turned her head so he could get a clear look at her ear and the side of her head where some of the hair had been unevenly cut away. Then he shook his head, clucked his tongue, and said, "Looks like you nearly lost your ear, young lady."

Rose nodded. "Other people lost a lot more than that."

The surgeon grabbed a staghorn-handled cane that was leaning against the desk and used it to leverage himself out of his worn leather chair. Then he took her head and said, "Come along, we'll take a look at your wounds," and hobbled out of the office and down a hallway to the next door down, leading her into a room with an examination bed along the wall. He bade her sit on it while he thoroughly washed his hands. Then he came to the examination table and took a close look at Rose's ear. She winced when he touched the pinna. "Hmm. That's a deep cut but it didn't quite reach the ear canal. It would be best if we stitched the upper ear back together." Then he examined the two gashes, now closed and caked with dried blood that laterally crossed the side of her skull. "The upper incision is approximately six inches in length, crossing in a shallow arc from the parietal to the frontal bone. The other is a straighter cut about four inches long, just missing the sphenoid. This is when your ear was cut. The person using the knife was applying downward pressure; the blade deflected off your skull and struck the pinna where it connects to your scalp at the top of the ear. The cuts pierced several layers of your scalp but I do not believe they were deep enough to affect the pericranium. Some major veins were severed I suspect, hence the copious amount of bleeding."

Eldemann straightened up and stood there, looking at her solemnly, arms folded. "I would say these wounds were inflicted upon you about four or five days ago."

Rose nodded.

"Well I don't believe we'll need to stitch your scalp. Those cuts have closed. The question that remains is if they are infected, but I do not see any sign of that. Still, the wounds need to cleaned thoroughly with iodine. I believe it would be best to use some chloroform and put you to sleep, young lady, while I do the cleaning and the stitching. It will be extremely painful if you choose to remain conscious."

"Will my hair grow back!?"

The surgeon nodded and smiled. "For the most part."

"Thank you. I'll take the chloroform." She was tired of hurting.

The surgeon bade her lay down on her back. She did so, pulling the blanket down to cover her from her shoulder blades to the top of her thighs. Eldemann placed what looked like a strainer with a wooden handle over her nose and then draped a thrice-folded cloth atop the cone-shaped wire. "The cloth will be soaked with chloroform," he explained, holding up a corked brown glass bottle for her to see. "It will smell faintly sweet. The cone keeps the soaked cloth off your skin, as otherwise the chloroform would burn your flesh. Just breathe slowly and deeply and in a few minutes you will drift off to sleep.

"How long will I be unconscious?"

"You will begin to wake up shortly after the cloth is taken away. Don't you fret. I've done this numerous times."

Rose closed her eyes as the surgeon began administering the chloroform, and breathed deeply, not at all sure if she cared whether she woke up or not.

* * *

When Rose awoke she was still lying on the examination table, covered with a blanket, and the whole side of her head was throbbing. She reached up and touched the tight clean dressing round her head. It covered her ear on that side, as well. Her throat was parched, and when she sat up the room tilted and spun slowly and she lay back down. She moaned softly and squeezed her eyes shut, and when she opened them again the old surgeon was there, standing by the table, smiling sympathetically. He gently cupped his hand behind her head and lifted it, bringing a spoon filled with a reddish-brown liquid to her lips.

"Laudanum," he said. "It took some time and a lot of scrubbing to get those wounds clean, and your ear required eight stitches. Here, drink this, it will numb the pain and help you sleep tonight."

Rose opened her mouth and he poured the spoonful of laudanum onto her tongue. She grimaced and swallowed it quickly. "That tastes awful!"

He helped her sit up and held onto her shoulder for a moment, as though he knew that she was suddenly dizzy even before she brought a hand up to her head, the other hand clutching the blanket against her body.

"How long since you had a decent meal, young lady?"

     JASON MANNING

Rose had to think about that. When one was in a living hell and the days seemed to drag on forever, almost as long as the nights, time was distorted and she had to think about it, finally determining that this was the third day out of Wild Horses. The only things she had eaten since the hide hunters had carried off were a couple of corn dodgers and a strip of dried meat that Sangre had given her. On the day of her abduction she had had breakfast. "Going on four days," she told the doctor.

Eldemann looked at the sergeant, who was leaning against a wall with arms folded. "I want you to take her to the post store and get her any fresh fruit they have there, and some cans of peaches. Tell the clerk to put it on my account."

"I can't do that, Doc. The captain told me to get her cleaned up, bring her to you, and then to take her back to her quarters."

Eldemann scowled in silence for a moment, looking from the sergeant to Rose and then back to the sergeant again.

"How did she come to be here, Sergeant?"

"Came in with a bunch of hide hunters. Their leader owed the captain some money. He didn't have quite enough so they threw this gal in to make up the difference. At least that's what I heard."

The surgeon was fuming. "So, the Captain is up to his old tricks again, is he?" He looked at Rose. "Where are your folks, young lady?"

Rose looked at him blankly. All she could really think about was how badly her head hurt. "I have no idea," she said.

Eldemann dug some coins out of his trouser pocket and went up to the sergeant, took the man's wrist and lifted his hand, turned it palm up and put the coins in it, then closed the sergeant's hand into a fist.

"If you have any decency in you, Sergeant, you will take this patient to the post store and do what I told you. Let her eat all she wants. Then for God's sake let her sleep."

The sergeant found he could not hold the doctor's gaze. He looked away sheepishly and coughed. "Okay, Doc. I'll do it."

"I will want to see her tomorrow."

The sergeant nodded. "I'll tell the Captain."

As the sergeant was escorting Rose out, Eldemann came up to

press the bottle of laudanum into her hand. "Take another spoonful today if you need to, and another in the morning, but no more than that."

Rose was beginning to feel the effects of the laudanum by the time they got to the post's store, where the sergeant was as good as his word. A quarter of an hour after leaving the infirmary, Rose was sitting at a table in the commandant's house, wolfing down the contents of a can of peach halves swimming in syrup. Her full stomach combined with the effects of the laudanum had her nodding off into an exhausted sleep. There was a point beyond which even anxiety and physical discomfort could not keep her awake.

*　*　*

When Rose awoke the next time it was slowly. Her eyelids fluttered first, but she didn't want to open her eyes. Then she murmured softly, and turned her head. She couldn't seem to roll over and eventually this registered and she wondered why. She tried again but couldn't seem to move her arms or legs very much at all. It took a while longer before this created a stir of anxiety.

"So, you're awake. Good."

Her eyes open. Her vision was blurry at first, but eventually she managed to focus on Telford. The captain was sitting in an armchair, a thick, leather-bound book open in his lap. He closed the book and placed it on a pedestal table by the chair. He sat there and looked at her with a faint curl on his knife-slit mouth, an elbow planted on the chair's arm, his thumb and forefinger grooming his thick mustache. "You slept for a couple of hours. I wasn't going to let you continue much longer. How do you feel?"

She realized she was lying on her belly in a four-poster bed, on a feather mattress. She didn't remember climbing into a bed — the last thing she recalled was catching herself drifting off to sleep at the table in the kitchen where she had eaten under the watchful eye of the sergeant. She realized next that her body was uncovered, and she tried to reach down for a sheet or blanket, but couldn't. Looking up, she saw

 JASON MANNING

that her wrists were bound with rope, and the ropes were secured to the bedposts. Her heart lurched in her chest and she looked over one shoulder and the other, to see that her legs were secured to the lower bedposts. She was spread-eagled and naked as the day she had been born. It took a good deal of willpower but she managed to look Telford in the eye.

"You don't look surprised," remarked Telford, smiling. "Your predecessor made quite a fuss when she woke up for the first time in that bed. She cursed me, though I could not tell you what she said, as she apparently did not speak a word of English. She was an Indian girl, you see. Her father had too many daughters it seems, and too little money for firewater. He sold her to a fellow who lost her to me in a game of five-card draw."

"Yes, you told me," said Rose. "Remember? You said she gave you some trouble and she died." Her voice was hoarse, but she was happy that she sounded quite calm for one shot through with anxiety.

Telford smiled and stood up, moved to the bed and sat on the edge. "Yes, indeed, she did. I was careless one day, and she got her hands on a knife and tried to stab me in the heart with it. As a consequence, I had her assigned to the non-commissioned officers' barracks as a maid. About two weeks later she hanged herself from a rafter." Telford shrugged. "I can't say that I was sorry. I'm sure they didn't treat her well there. But she brought it on herself. She tried to kill me and she was as well off as someone like her could expect to be while under this roof."

Rose lay there a moment struggling to tamp down the panic trying to take her over as she realized that this man was a cold-blooded bastard

"So that's why you took me."

Telford nodded, and reached out. Rose tensed and her tense body jumped when his hand came to rest on the small of her back. He left it there, as he said, "That is correct. Although you were quite a mess I could see beneath the blood and the filth. You are a very pretty young woman. Much prettier than the worn-out whores you find in the tent town. Much prettier than any Indian woman I have seen. And I like to have a young, pretty woman around. I am married but my wife refused to come with me when I was posted out here. I have asked her several times since, in letters that I have sent. She has continued to refuse. So if anyone is to blame for you being here it is her." He let his hand roam up the smooth slope of her thigh, and she stiffened. "You *are* a whore, aren't you? That's what that pig, Kelleren, called you. That's why they brought you with them from that town, Wild Horses, isn't it? That and the likelihood that you were the prettiest girl there."

His mention of Wild Horses reminded her of the lies Kelleren had told this man. "He lied to you. Kelleren did. The mountain man didn't go around killing everyone. It was his hide hunters that started it." She decided not to go into details about what Morris had done to her, and how Eldon Caulfield had died trying to save her. That was entirely too painful and she didn't want to cry in the presence of this man.

Telford let his hand roam up the supple curve of her back and then he grabbed her by the hair and yanked hard. She cried out in pain. He leaned down and hissed.

"You have no business concerning yourself with such things, girl. But let me tell you, it doesn't matter what really happened. What matters is what is *going* to happen. Kelleren will tell his story from here to the Apacheria and folks with believe that this mountain man, this Lobo Riler, is a cold-blooded killer. Then they will know that Captain John Telford was the man who brought Riler to justice. You say otherwise and you may lose your tongue. You understand me?"

Rose hissed a pain-tinged "Yes!" through clenched teeth.

Telford stood up and began unbuckling his belt, grinning at her. Rose turned her face away, her uneasy stomach doing a slow roll. She expected him to cover her now, to have his way with his new prize. Instead he began to whip her with the belt, hard and with enthusiasm. She screamed hoarsely as the leather bit into her flesh. Her body arched and shuddered and flopped as the searing pain consumed her. The whipping lasted but a handful of seconds, until there were eight angry welts across her back from her shoulder blades to her upper thighs.

Then Rose felt the mattress sag under the captain's weight, and

  JASON MANNING

squeezed her eyes closed, tears running down her cheeks. *You deserve this*, she told herself. *This is what you get for the deeds you've done. This is God's punishment for your sins and nobody is going to save you.*

Three days later, Lobo Riler arrived.

CHAPTER 18

The ride to Fort Laramie nearly killed him.

When he stopped his buckskin and with bleak, pain-reddened eyes scanned the bluff that was covered by Fort Laramie and then the sprawling tent town adjacent to it, Lobo Riler was sitting his saddle hunched at the shoulders, a white-knuckled grip on the saddlehorn. It was just after daybreak — there were still a few stars holding out in the dark blue sky behind him — while a riot of pink and orange and yellow above the eastern horizon straight ahead was becoming bright enough that he had to squint.

Gus Freeman checked his swaybacked sorrel mare alongside the buckskin, spared the fort and tent town a cursory glance before turning worried eyes at Riler, then at the bandage wrapped tightly around the mountain man's midsection. There were large bloodstains on it, and more on the homespun shirt he wore under his serape. His deerskin tunic had been too soaked with blood to clean, and Julie Regret had given him the shirt. Gus figured it had been Moke Regret's shirt.

Julie had given Gus extra bandages and a bottle of laudanum for

Riler, who had certainly needed the former, as his wounds had reopened the first day out of Wild Horses. Gus had applied fresh bandaging but Riler had refused to take a drop of the laudanum. By now Gus was tempted to, though. It had been a hard ride, because Riler wasn't one to dally, even when wracked with pain. The mountain man had been of the opinion that it figured that it would take Kelleren and his crew the better part of three days to reach the Laramie River, even if they were in a hurry. The mule teams would pull those hide-laden wagons only so fast. It had taken Riler and the blacksmith just two days.

"Lobo, you might ought to let me check and wash your wounds while we're here at the river, and then I can put a new bandage on you."

Riler shook his head. "I want to know how long ago Kelleren passed through." He looked down at the wolfdog, who had come loping up to drink at the river's edge.

Gus looked anxiously across the river and this time scanned the tent town, which seemed to be just now waking up. He saw the plumes of woodsmoke from a dozen campfires and a handful of figures moving here and there through the makeshift structures. "What if him and his cutthroats are still there?"

Riler smiled coldly. "That would be nice," he rasped, and kicked the buckskin forward into the river's shallows. The Laramie was running high and fast thanks to snowmelt, but the course was shallow enough here that swimming the horses wasn't required. Riler was relieved, figuring that the frigid water and the strong current might prove too much for him in his present state.

When they reached the eastern embankment they dismounted and led their horses into the tent town. Apart from the residents — the traders and the merchants and the prostitutes — there were some settlers pausing on their way westward, and some Indians looking to trade pelts for trinkets and old smoothbore muskets and — in some cases — cheap whiskey. People were gathered round morning fires to warm themselves or cook up some breakfast. Some of them looked up curiously at the two men leading their horses — and at the wolfdog that accompanied them. Riler caught a whiff of strong coffee and had a hankering, but he pressed on, hoping against hope that he would see Kelleren or one of his crew. As he made his way around a shanty made of broken planks, driftwood and old blankets, leading the buckskin and with Gus trailing along behind, he felt a tug on the sleeve of his shirt and heard someone say "You want buy *wasicun?*" Riler caught a glimpse of a scalp dangled briefly in front of his face. He turned, pulling free of the grasping fingers and was about to issue an ill-tempered threat when he recognized the grinning face of Dohasan.

"Well, I'll be damned," said Riler, astonished. "You're still above snakes!"

"And *you* are alive, Mister Riler!" exclaimed the delighted Indian youth. Then he saw the bloodstained bandages around the mountain man's midsection and his smile faded. "Lucky to *be* alive, looks like."

"We thought for sure you'd be kilt when you lit out after them hide hunters," said Gus Freeman. "You should know I buried your father out in the tall grass near my Smoking Woman."

Dohasan's expression was bleak, his eyes dark. "I wanted to kill them all, but they stayed too close together most of the time. The first night one of them rode back along their trail. I tried to sneak up on him but he had good ears, or good instincts, or both. I couldn't get close enough to kill him with my knife before he could shoot me and I didn't dare use the shotgun."

"And what of Rose?" asked Riler.

"She's alive. But that hide hunter named McNally isn't." He said it with a fierce jubilation. "When my father went out into the street, McNally was trying to reach you. I think he intended to take your scalp. My father shot his legs out from under him … right before he died…."

Riler grimaced. Already badly wounded and face down in the street, he had seen none of what Dohasan was now telling him. The way he saw it, he owed a debt to Seth Topper, and since Seth was dead that obligation passed to his adopted son.

"…So he needed a doctor, and the other hide hunters left him here to get his legs seen to. I followed him as he rode around, asking people if there was a doctor and he finally found one. I saw him go into a tent not far from where we stand. I watched and waited. The doctor left and I slipped in. McNally was unconscious. I slit his throat, and took this." He proudly held up the scalp.

"For the love of God, boy," said Freeman, aghast at the cold-blooded elation evident in Dohasan's tone and expression.

The young Sioux glared at the blacksmith. "They killed my *ate-ki* — my father! They almost killed Mister Riler. They are all killers, and they all deserve to die. Why are you here if you do not believe that?"

Freeman thought about it a moment, brows furrowed. "Well, I ain't much good with a pistol or rifle, I confess, and I don't know the first thing about fightin' with a knife. So I don't know that I'm much good at all, to tell the truth, 'less one of 'em wants to arm wrassle."

Riler looked sternly at Dohasan. "He's here because he thinks he should be. Just like you are. You said Kelleren and the others left. When, and in what direction did they go?'

"Two days ago. They headed east. They' are hunting more *ta-tanka*." He glanced at Freeman. "Buffalo."

Freeman nodded, smiling. "I know. You're forgettin' I had me an Injun wife."

"And Rose. Is she with them?" asked Riler.

"No. Kelleren sold her to a captain. His name is Telford. He runs the fort."

"*Sold* her?"

Dohasan nodded. "First he sold his hides to a trader. I saw him. Then soldiers came. They surrounded the wagons. I could not get close enough to hear everything that was said without being seen. But I do know that the captain sold Kelleren the wagons and mules he uses. That was two winters ago and Kelleren didn't come back last year to finish paying off his debt. When the captain found out he was here *this* year, he brought some soldiers with him. They surrounded the wagons. The captain told Kelleren he wanted all that was owed him, or else. I saw Kelleren give the captain all the money he had just been paid. It wasn't enough to settle the debt though, so when the captain said he would take Rose to settle it, Kelleren agreed. Then Kelleren begged the captain for enough of the money back so he could pay his men. Said they would go hunt another load of hides and then square things with the captain once and for all."

"Why would this captain care if Kelleren paid his men?" asked Riler.

Dohasan shrugged. "Maybe because he thought that if he didn't then the hide hunters would start trouble and there would be bloodshed."

Riler rubbed his stubbled chin and thought about it a moment, then nodded. "Maybe so. Collecting that debt was his personal business."

"Makes sense," added Freeman. "If soldiers died, how would he explain that?"

"You mean justify it," said Dohasan. The look on the blacksmith's face made him smile. It felt odd to smile. It had been a long time since he had done so. "My father spent a couple of hours a day, every day, teaching me to read and write and speak in English," he said defensively.

"Reckon you've got more book-learnin' than me," allowed Freeman. "My master freed me but he didn't learn me any of that. He said white folk were afraid of free blacks, but would be even more afraid of free, educated blacks."

"My *ate-ki* said the same thing about educated Indians. But he taught me anyway."

"You saw Rose," said Riler. "How did she look?"

"She looked tired and dirty and…."

"And what?"

"Hopeless."

"That captain might have done what he did to save Miss Rose from Kelleren and his men," suggested Freeman, glancing at Riler.

"No," said Dohasan. "Rose was wearing a blanket and nothing else. The captain made her open the blanket so he could get a look at her. He touched her. He hankered after her, that was clear. To have her, not to save her."

Freeman looked worried. He could read the expression on Riler's face and had a bad feeling that the mountain man was going to let emotions cloud his judgment and go off and do something reckless and maybe get himself killed. And maybe him and Dohasan, too. The blacksmith tried to change the subject. He looked at Dohasan. "So Kelleren is comin' back here." Then he looked at Riler. "Are we gonna wait for him here, Lobo?"

"Maybe," said Riler, though his thoughts were not on the hide hunters but rather on Rose Waldron. She was here, now, and he was going to get her back. "Where was Rose taken?"

The young Sioux shrugged. "Into the fort, I guess. But I didn't follow. I was watching the hide hunters Kelleren paid his men and told McNally he would have to stay and get his wounds looked after. He said they would be back in a month, maybe less."

Riler looked north, in the direction of the bluff that loomed over the shanty town. "I better go find out if she's okay." He knew even as he said it that this would not be enough, that he was going to take her back to Wild Horses, come hell or high water.

Freeman put a hand on his shoulder. "Let me go, Lobo."

"Why you?"

Freeman shrugged. "Nobody will pay me no mind. I'll find out where she is, and then we can maybe come up with a plan to get her free."

"There's no 'maybe' about that," said Riler.

"If Dohasan heard right, there'll be trouble for sure if you go up there lookin' the way you do."

"You can't go up there, Mister Riler," said Dohasan. He, too, could tell how deeply troubled the mountain man was.

"And why the hell can't I?" asked Riler, belligerently. His tone of voice agitated the wolfdog, who abruptly stood up. He looked around, black lips peeling back from its fangs, then studied both Freeman and Dohasan, its nose twitching, trying to gauge whether either one of them posed a threat to its master.

For this reason, Dohasan answered Riler's question in a quiet, friendly tone that seemed incongruous as he murmured, "Because Kelleren told the captain that you had killed a bunch of people in Wild Horses. That you went loco and killed three of his men and some of the town folk, too, and that he and his men had run off."

Both Riler and Freeman were startled by this news. "That son of a bitch," muttered the former.

"Guess Kelleren knew you wasn't dead when he hightailed it out of Wild Horses," said Freeman. "And that since you wasn't, you'd be comin' after him. He wants that captain to take care of you for him. But why would the captain believe him?"

"I don't think he did," said Dohasan. "He said something like the truth depended on who was left standing."

Riler nodded. "The truth of it doesn't matter to him. All he cares about is getting all the money he thinks Kelleren owes him. He won't think twice about killing me to make sure that I don't kill Kelleren before the debt is paid."

"Then maybe we should get out of here," suggested Freeman.

Riler looked at him, blue eyes cold as steel. "I'm not leaving here without Rose," he rasped.

Freeman sighed. He was a man who knew his shortcomings. He wasn't a particularly brave man, but the thought of turning tail and abandoning Riler wasn't a palatable one. There was only one way he could see to keep the mountain man from throwing away his life trying to rescue Rose Waldron.

"Let me go up there," he begged Riler. "Give me a chance to get her out before you go and get your head shot off."

"Let him try, Mister Riler," urged Dohasan.

Riler looked up at the top of the bluff once more. He realized that the odds of his finding Rose and getting her away from the fort were very long, but he was not accustomed to letting others risk their lives on his account. He even gave some thought to telling both Dohasan and the blacksmith to hightail it back to Wild Horses. But he had a hunch neither one of them would leave.

He took a deep breath and let it out in a gusting sigh, then nodded curtly at Freeman, much to the relief of both the blacksmith and the Sioux youth.

"Okay. You go. But if you're not back by sundown I'm coming in to get both you and Rose, you hear?"

     JASON MANNING

Freeman nodded and tried to put a brave smile on his face. Without a word walked off in the direction of Fort Laramie.

Riler turned to Dohasan. "Where's your horse?"

"South of this place is the camp of a small group of Cheyenne. Most of them stay drunk. But the people here won't go near them, since they're Indians. That's where I left my horse."

"Do you know any of them?"

Dohasan shook his head. "They are all outcasts. They have been made foolish by the white man's firewater. They have no pride. They won't steal my horse, though, or try to sell him."

"Why not?"

"Because of these." Dohasan lifted McNally's scalp, and touched the shotgun dangling by down his back. "Come, I will take you there. We should stay among the Cheyenne until Gus gets back."

Riler nodded. "Lead the way." He looked back at the bluff once more, thinking about Rose, wondering what she was having to endure — then tried not to think about it. He glanced at the sun and grimaced. It was going to be a long day of waiting and wondering.

CHAPTER 19

The Cheyenne camp on the outskirts of the Laramie tent town consisted of only a half-dozen skin lodges and Riler counted sixteen residents, which including several children. When he and Dohasan showed up, two of the men came to meet them. The rest kept their distance, except for a little boy who obviously just learned to walk — until his mother rushed forward and swept the boy into her arms, glancing at Riler apprehensively as she hurried away.

Riler knew plenty about the Cheyenne language since he had lived with one for years, but he said nothing, letting Dohasan do the talking. Dohasan told their welcoming committee that he was a friend of his in particular and Indians in general. He didn't mention Quahneah, though he knew about her, and Riler understood why, Many Indians did not appreciate the fact that a number of mountain men had wooed, bought, or stolen Indian women to warm their blankets.

While this went on Riler didn't fail to notice how the two Cheyenne braves were looking over his horse, saddle, rifle, and wolfdog companion. Despite what Dohasan had said about these people not

         JASON MANNING

being thieves he was on his guard and in the mood for trouble. The two braves saw this, as well, and soon they were smiling affably and inviting him and Dohasan to sit by their fire, where the women were cooking what looked to Riler to be a medium-sized dog, skinned and roasting on an iron spit. While he was cold clean through and his empty stomach felt like it was tied up in a painful knot, he chose to unsaddle his horse first, then hobbled it so it wouldn't wander far. The buckskin moved just out of the Cheyenne camp and began pawing at the thin crust of snow in search of new grass. Riler was confident that anyone who tried to lead the buckskin too far from its owner or to mount it would regret the attempt. In addition, the wolfdog was as protective when it came to Riler's possessions as it was when it came to the mountain man himself.

He figured these Cheyennes were outcasts from their tribe and that they survived here by stealing or hunting, selling the fresh meat to a tent town population that was in constant need of it. In this day of rising animosity between white men and red, they tried to live on the edge of a knife.

Only after the horse was taken care of did Riler settle by the fire, sitting with a groan, tenderly holding his side, an arm wrapped around his midsection. One of the Cheyenne men — there were five that sat around the fire — offered to tend to his wound but Riler thanked him for the offer and shook his head. One of the women offered him a piece of dog meat and he accepted it gratefully, wolfing it down. He told Dohasan to wake him at once if Gus Freeman showed up, then lay down and put an arm over his eyes — the sun was halfway to its zenith and the sky was clear. He fell into an exhausted sleep, the wolfdog lying right beside him.

When he awoke the sun was halfway down the western sky. It surprised him that he had slept at least four hours. He hadn't slept that well since the last night in his cabin high up in the Medicine Bow Mountains. He lay there a moment, feeling better than he had since the street fight in Wild Horses. That lasted until he sat up, then he winced at a stabbing pain. He noticed then he wore a clean dressing.

"I thought it was a good time to change that," said Dohasan, coming into view and sitting on his heels beside the mountain man. "These people gave me some medicine and I put it on your wounds. It looked like there was an infection setting in. The poultice should draw it out."

"Obliged," said Riler, gratefully, as he looked around in hopes of seeing Gus Freeman — and even Rose Waldron. But all he saw were Cheyenne, watching him until he looked at them, and then they would look away. "No sign of Gus, then."

Dohasan shook his head. "Not yet. But it is a big fort, Mister Riler."

Riler shook his head. He had a bad feeling. But then he'd had one ever since he had set out after the hide hunters, and barely able to stay in the saddle to boot. He checked the sun and calculated there were a few more hours of daylight remaining.

"If he's not back by dark I'm going in to find him and Rose," he told Dohasan with a tone that made clear he would brook no argument.

Dohasan nodded. "She might be okay. Maybe she won't even want to leave. Maybe that captain is taking care of her." He saw the anger in Riler's eyes and shrugged. "I mean she is just a whore after all. It seems she is only interested in one thing."

Riler managed to keep his anger in check, only out of respect for his friend, Seth Topper. "If she doesn't want to leave then I won't make her. But I'm going to find out if she wants to."

Dohasan glanced to the east, at the rolling sea of grass to the east, which he could see between two of the Cheyenne skin lodges. "I just think we should go after the hide hunters and settle that. You could check on her on the way back."

"Except we might not come back."

Dohasan thought about that and nodded. "I'm not afraid to die." He wasn't trying to reassure Riler. It was just a statement of fact.

"The thing is, if Rose is in a bad situation and we ride off and get ourselves killed, she doesn't get out of it." Riler glanced in the direction of the bluff on which Fort Laramie was perched. "And now that may go for Gus, too." He laid back down and sighed with relief. The paste

          JASON MANNING

that the Cheyenne had made seemed to have had a quick and positive effect on his pain. He guessed that it included yarrow, and perhaps locoweed, but it didn't really matter. It worked, and that was enough. "I'm going to rest some more," he told Dohasan, and in minutes was again fast asleep.

* * *

That night, Lobo Riler roamed the tents and shanties of the town below the bluff. Freeman had not returned, and he was determined to slip into the fort and find both him and Rose. He wasn't about to lose another friend if he could help it.

He had left the wolfdog back in the Cheyenne encampment, knowing it would stay close to the buckskin and there was nothing anyone could do to lure him away. Also left behind was the Sharps rifle. His plan was to pass himself off as a soldier, and a soldier wouldn't be roaming around the fort with a rifle in hand unless he was on guard duty. He didn't plan on taking on the entire garrison anyway. A knife and his Colt Navy would suffice.

He had told Dohasan to remain with the outcast Indians and Topper's adopted son hadn't even asked to accompany him. Riler didn't hold that against him. He understood that Dohasan had no quarrel with the bluecoats, being single-minded in his obsession with doing away with Kelleren and the other hide hunters. Besides, Riler had a plan for slipping into Fort Laramie and his being accompanied by an Indian youth or a wolfdog would make that plan unworkable.

Figuring that soldiers garrisoned in the fort would visit the tent town to find whiskey and women, he prowled in the shadows looking for a place that offered both amenities. It didn't take long for him to find one. From some distance he heard a fiddle being played, accompanied by loud, drunken voices. These sounds issued from a large tent with three wooden walls fashioned from roughly hewn lumber. The interior gleamed with the reddish-gold light of lanterns. Standing outside in the night shadows — the moon would not rise for another couple of hours — he studied the men inside. An old man was working behind the makeshift bar — some boards placed across barrels while a couple of scantily clad women carried drinks to patrons who sat on stools or crates or a few rickety chairs round several tables. Blankets dangled from a rope run from one side wall to the other, sectioning off the back of the tent where, considering the sounds that issued from the other side of the blankets, at least one woman was entertaining at least two men. Finding a place about ten strides away where he could hunker down and probably not be seen by men who emerged from the lighted interior, he picked a likely target among the half-dozen soldiers he could see inside the makeshift saloon — and waited.

He had to wait a while. A pair of soldiers left the makeshift saloon, and while they were drunk enough that they stumbled and swayed as they walked away, Riler was not inclined to take on more than one if he could help it. That would just double the chances of an alarm being raised. He tried to put Gus and Rose out of his mind, to stop thinking about how long this was taking, to stop considering time at all, even though he preferred to get done what had to be done before moonrise. He also ignored the bitter cold that crept into his bones. He wore only the homespun shirt which Julie Regret had given him to replace his deerskin tunic. He had left the serape behind in the Cheyenne encampment.

Then it happened, a single soldier, large in frame, wearing an army-issue overcoat and a woolen scarf against the cold, who entered the saloon and, much to Riler's delight, paid for a bottle of rotgut whiskey and then left. Riler waited until the man disappeared between two tents, and then rose and followed in his quarry's footsteps, quiet as a mouse. The soldier pulled the cork out of the bottle with his teeth and began to drink. Riler waited until he was certain no one was close enough to see and then closed in with long strides, drawing the Colt Navy revolver from under his belt, flipping it so he could grasp the barrel and then raised it, so that when his left arm went between the soldier's arm and upper torso and his hand throttled the man's throat, he could bring the butt of the revolver down on his target's skull. The bottle of whiskey landed with a thump on the hard-packed ground and began to spill its contents as the soldier slumped. Riler lowered himself to one knee so he could let the unconscious man down quietly, wincing because supporting the other's weight stressed his wound.

Once he had the man down, Riler rolled him over on his stomach and stripped the overcoat off of him. Brandishing a length of rope he had borrowed from the Cheyenne, he tied the wrist and ankle bindings together, so that the fallen soldier could not get to his feet when he regained consciousness. Then he used the threadbare scarf to gag the man.

Getting to his feet, he donned the overcoat and the man's forage cap, pulled the brim down low over his face, secured the Navy revolver under his belt and picked up the fallen whiskey bottle. There were a few fingers worth of who-hit-john still in it and he poured it all over the overcoat. Then he took a long careful look around. It seemed the assault had gone unnoticed. He wondered how long the soldier would remain unconscious. In his experience, it could be a matter of seconds or perhaps minutes. There was no way of knowing for sure — and no time to waste. He could only hope that, bound and gagged as he was, the man would not be able to bring attention to his plight right away.

A road wide enough for wagons had been graded on the southern slope of the bluff and up this he walked, or rather stumbled like a drunken man. It was fortunate that there was no perimeter wall around Fort Laramie, but at the top of the grade was a sentry who, from his vantage point, had a view of the tent town below. Riler pulled the collar of the overcoat up and stuffed his hands in its pockets, humming "John Brown's Body" — the tune Freeman had been humming the day he had arrived in Wild Horses.

The sentry, standing perhaps twenty feet away, watched him with some amusement, and as he reached the top of the grade and said, "Too much too fast of that snakehead they sell down there will curl your toes." Riler grunted and made a dismissive gesture and kept moving, realizing that he should have known the man he had waylaid had probably past this same soldier on his way down into the tent town. He heard the sentry chuckle as he passed between two buildings and found himself on the edge of a parade ground circled by one- and two-story structures, some dark, others with golden lamplight glowing in the windows.

He had never had reason to visit Fort Laramie and knew nothing about its interior. He saw four cannons arrayed around a flagpole in the center of the parade ground. Turning left, he began walking, without the drunkard's shuffle, but soon veered off at an angle across the open ground — as soon as he realized he was approaching a row of barracks and that there were a few men out on the front porch of the first one — he saw the orange glow of a cigar's burning tip, and then a burst of laughter. He was well aware that he would be seen quartering the parade ground and could only hope no one would find it remarkable.

While he walked, head down, eyes darting this way and that, he wondered how he could find the commandant's residence, relying on the assumption that he would find Rose there. As for Gus Freeman's whereabouts, he couldn't even guess where the Wild Horses blacksmith might be. It seemed likely that he would be found out before he located either of the people he had come for. And by now the man he had knocked out was most likely conscious. He expected to hear shouts of alarm at any moment. The odds against him were mighty high and would get higher still if he was found to be posing as the soldier he had assaulted.

Nearing the western edge of the parade ground he saw a soldier standing guard at the door of an adobe building some distance away, and angled immediately into the deeper night shadow between two more adobe structures, both of them dark and quiet. He circled around behind them and reached the back of the building that was guarded. He saw only one window, and it was crosshatched with iron bars. A dim light came through the window. He approached it cautiously, peeked inside.

It was a cellblock, with four cells on either side and a closed, iron-reinforced door opposite the window some thirty feet away. A soldier was sprawled on a narrow cot in one of the cells on the left, snoring loudly. In the cell directly across from the snorer was a shape covered by a blanket on another cot. He couldn't make out more than that in the weak light cast by an oil lantern turned down low and hanging on

     JASON MANNING

a nail next to the door.

Was Gus Freeman the man under the blanket? The guard at the front of the building was as close as twenty-five feet away, so calling out — or even a loud whisper — would betray his presence on this quiet night. The size of the cellblock compared to the measurements of the building made him certain there was another room up front, and he had no way of knowing if there was anyone present in that room, as there were no other windows on this wall. He assumed if the front room had a window it was on the side of the building.

Putting his back to the wall he considered his options. If he took out the guard and managed to enter the building and it wasn't Gus sleeping under that blanket then his chances of finding Rose — and of even getting out of the fort in one piece — would be greatly reduced. But Riler had already decided that the only reason Freeman hadn't come back out of the fort was that he was either confined or dead. He considered forgetting about Gus and just trying to find the commandant's quarters. But the code of frontier honor he had learned from trappers like Topper, and that he tried to live by for all his years in the mountains, wouldn't allow him to make that choice.

He pushed off from the wall, stuffed the nearly empty bottle of whiskey into the left side pocket of the stolen overcoat, and circled back around the adjacent building to step out into view and turn left. Then he began stumbling slightly again and slipped one hand under his coat, fingertips touching the butt of the Colt Navy. He kept his head down so that the brim of the forage cap would conceal much of his face. Unless he was asleep the guard had to have seen him after a few steps but said nothing. Riler fought the urge to look up just in case there was a rifle aimed at him until he was close enough to see the guard's booted feet.

Right then the guard chuckled. "Little too much bravemaker, eh?"

Riler turned his head to the right for a quick scan of the parade ground, saw no one, and then lifted his head as he pulled the bottle out of the pocket with his left hand while his right slipped off the butt of the pistol under his belt. He gestured with that hand, to make sure the soldier noticed it was empty. "Yeah. Too much too fast. Finish it for me?" He held out the bottle, swaying. The guard was looking at the bottle rather than his face, and then he too scanned his surroundings before leaning the Spencer carbine against the front wall of the brig. While reaching for the bottle he looked up to meet Riler's gaze, and his brows were just beginning to furrow as he realized he didn't recognize the face under the brim of the forage cap when the mountain man's fist smashed into his face.

CHAPTER 20

Catching the unconscious guard as he began to crumple, Riler pinned him with his weight against the front wall and swiftly checked all his pockets for a key. There wasn't one. The mountain man grimaced. He wasn't really surprised. That would have been too easy. He stepped away and let the body drop, and then reached out to knock over the carbine, before pressing his back against the wall to the right of the door, the Colt Navy still in hand.

It was another gamble — that since the guard didn't have a key, and therefore no way to check on the two prisoners, then there was at least a chance that someone else was inside. Riler didn't have to wait long to find out if his hunch was correct. He heard the clatter and click of a key in a lock and the door swung open. Hitting it with his shoulder, he threw it open and in the process sent the soldier who had unlocked it sprawling on his back. Riler kicked the door shut. The key was still in the lock. He turned it, locking the door, and pocketed the key. The soldier was laying there, eyes wide and staring at the Navy Colt. There was a rivulet of blood running out of his nose.

"D-don't shoot," he stammered.

"Don't be a fool and I won't have to."

"Who are you? Wh-what do you want?"

"Looking for a man, former slave, now a blacksmith, name of Gus Freeman. Is he here?"

The soldier didn't reply, and Riler could tell he was starting to think again, so he cocked the Colt Navy. That encouraged the soldier to hastily nod in response.

"Good. Now you're going to get up and go back there and let him out."

As he slowly got to his feet, the soldier wiped at his nose and looked at the blood on his fingers and asked, "You're not going to kill me, are you?"

"Not unless you make me."

The soldier nodded and turned, unwilling to take his eyes off the pistol in Riler's hand. He got a ring of keys off a nail beside the cell block door, unlocked the door and went inside. Riler followed. Freeman stirred when he heard the key in the cell door's lock and when he saw Riler he jumped to his feet, a look of amazement on his face. Riler put a finger to his lip before the blacksmith could blurt something, like his name. The soldier opened the cell door and when Freeman was out Riler motioned for the soldier to get in.

"I won't make a sound, I promise," said the soldier as he entered the cell.

"I know you won't," said Riler, and grabbed the front of the soldier's shirt, saw the fear gleam in the man's eyes and then struck once with the pistol, knocking the man out cold and easing him down onto the cot. Then he left the cell and locked it, checked the prisoner in the other cell, who was still snoring away, and at this range Riler could detect the smell of whiskey.

"I done failed you again," sighed Freeman, looking as downcast as a person could look. "I ain't worth much of nothin'."

Riler motioned for Gus to follow him into the front room, closed the cellblock door, and then asked, "Did you find out where Rose is?"

Freeman nodded. "I told the guard I run into that I was a

     JASON MANNING

blacksmith in need of work. He didn't believe me at first but I managed to convince him and he let me pass, told me to look up a feller
named Sanderson, who turned out to be one of the post blacksmiths.
That feller gave me some work to do and once I done it he took me
to the captain named Telford, in his office. But that captain wouldn't
agree to let me work in this here fort since I wasn't enlisted. Sanderson
sent me off to the mess hall to get some food and then told me to
leave. I got the food but I didn't leave. I found a spot where I could
watch the captain's office. An hour later he came out and I followed
him to his quarters. Found a place I could hide and watch, and when
he left I tried to get inside, but the door was locked and I was climbin'
through a window when a soldier caught me. That's how I ended up
in here. I kept tellin' 'em I was just lookin' for food for my family down
in the tent town. They think I'm just a thief."

Riler didn't waste time scolding Freeman for not leaving once he
had located Telford's quarters. Instead, he took the blacksmith by the
arm and led him outside. "Point me in the direction."

Freeman pointed north. "Right next to that big house they call
Old Bedlam."

"Get going. Leave the fort. Find the Cheyenne camp on the edge
of town."

Freeman nodded, dejected. "Reckon I'll go. Ain't much use to
you."

Riler clamped a hand down on the blacksmith's shoulder. "You've
been a big help, Gus."

He grabbed the unconscious guard by the ankles and dragged him
inside. When he was done he closed the door, locked it, and tossed the
key into the darkness. Freeman watched him do all this. "Go on," he
told the blacksmith. "Get out of here. If I don't come back with Rose
you head to Wild Horses. Tell Julie Regret what happened. At least
she'll know Rose is still alive. Now GO!"

Freeman went around the corner of the brig and disappeared into
the night.

* * *

When Riler reached the commandant's quarters all hell broke loose.

The commotion came from the direction of the brig, the shouts of several men followed by three gunshots, spaced well apart, which Riler assumed were meant to wake everyone in the fort. Either one of the two men he had knocked out had regained consciousness, or the unconscious soldiers had been discovered. Having circled around the long, two-story headquarters building, he broke into a run, making for Telford's house. As he came out from behind Old Bedlam he saw several men off to his right, making for the same destination at a run. They were close enough to see him, or at least his shape, had they looked his way, so he dropped to the ground and lay there, hoping the night shadows would conceal his form.

He heard the clomping of bootheels on the front porch of Telford's house as the three soldiers reached their destination. Since they were no longer in sight, Riler jumped to his feet and ran to the side of the clapboard structure that was reserved for the Laramie commander's use. He noticed then that the building stood on low adobe brick piers. He didn't hesitate to lie on his belly and crawl underneath the floor. It was a tight fit but he was completely out of sight now, and close enough to the front of the house to hear the door open on rusty hinges and a stern, gruff voice demanding to know what the commotion was about. Riler assumed that this was Telford.

"A prisoner has escaped, Captain!" exclaimed one breathless soldier.

"More like someone came and broke him out, Sir," blurted another. "Whoever did it knocked out Private Weller and Sergeant Stone, too."

"What prisoner?"

"That thievin' darky, Captain," said a third man.

After a moment of thought, Telford rasped, "I assume Stone and Weller will live."

"Reckon, so, sir," replied the third man.

"The prisoner is no longer in the fort, I'm sure," said Telford, "and it's unlikely we can find him in the dark. Let it go. He is of no consequence. Back to your posts or your beds, and don't bother me again

 JASON MANNING

unless all the tribes of the Northern Plains are descending on this damn fort."

The 'yes, sir's from the trio of soldiers all sounded surprised and disappointed. Riler heard them walking away and heard the front door close, and then the creak and thump of the captain's booted feet on the floor planking. He wondered briefly about the man he had waylaid in the tent town, and what the response would be should he show up. But there was little to be gained by worrying about that now. He was close to his goal and there was no time to waste. He crawled out from under the house and went around to the front. The three soldiers were nowhere to be seen. The fort was quieting down. He crept up onto the porch, putting his weight down slowly with each step as he moved to the door, thinking that he had not heard a lock being thrown. He tried the latch and breathed a soft "Huh" as the door opened — slowly, as he remembered how the hinges had squeaked when it had been opened moments ago and applied slight upward pressure on the latch to take some weight off the hinges.

The front room was spacious and well-furnished, dark but for the glow of a fire left to die hours before, reduced now to glowing embers in a pile of black ash and the charred remnants of several logs in a fireplace. He moved silent as a ghost across the untrustworthy floor, treading lightly, making sure his weight was supported by more than one plank at any one moment. Reaching a short hallway, he saw a door to his left that was closed and one to his right that was ajar. This one he opened slightly, enough to survey the room beyond. It too was dark, but his eyes were accustomed to the darkness now, and the first threads of moonlight were coming through a curtain-less window — enough light for him to see a shape under the covers on the bed across the room. His nostrils flared as he took a slow, steady, deep breath, remembering the perfume that, with the scent of sex, had permeated Rose Waldron's room at the Regret that day he had shared it with her. He didn't smell any perfume, though, and for the first time wondered if she was here, after all.

But he didn't hesitate, slipping through the opening and moving silently to the side of the bed, close enough now to hear breathing —

two people breathing. One was awake. Then he saw the ropes tied to the iron headboard and at the end of one of them a woman's hand, slowly closing into a fist — and then a glimpse of hair the color of spun-gold in the darkness, and he grabbed the covers with his left hand, filled the right with the Navy Colt, and as he threw back the covers and Telford started and then began to sit up, for the fourth time that night pistol-whipped a man. The captain grunted and fell back and Riler saw Rose's face then, the mouth opening, and he clamped his left hand over it and put the barrel of the Colt up to his lips as he would have a finger — had he had a finger free.

Shoving the Colt under his belt he drew his knife and leaned over to cut Rose free. She rose up and launched herself over Telford's unconscious body and into Riler's arms, sobbing as she buried her face in the stolen overcoat he wore. He wrapped his arms around her tightly, gratefully. He had not been a man who conferred much with the Almighty, but a heartfelt "Thank God!" escaped his lips at that moment.

"I didn't think you would come for me!" Rose sobbed, clinging to him tightly, as though afraid that if she loosened her grip he would vanish like a dream. "I-I didn't even know if you were still alive. But you are and yes! Thank God for that!" She noticed him studying the bandage around her head and sighed. "That black son of a bitch named Morris did this to me. I'm not pretty anymore."

"The hell you aren't," said Riler. Seeing her here and now made him feel even more guilty. Even in the dim illumination of moonlight filtering through one of the windows he could see her wrists, rubbed nearly raw by the rope with which she had been bound, and a few prominent bruises on her pale body. He pried her off and turned to the bed. He used the rope bindings to tie Telford to the bed, tore off a long strip of linen from a sheet and gagged the captain. Then he gathered up a quilt. "Let's get you out of here," he said gruffly.

"How are you going to do that?" she asked, despair putting a raw edge on her words. "I'm sure by now every soldier here knows about me."

Riler draped the quilt around her slender body not once but twice, snugly, her arms pinned to her sides. "You let me worry about that."

Rose glanced at the unconscious man sprawled on the bed. "Kill him," she said, and she looked at Telford with more hate in her eyes and in her voice than Riler had seen or heard in a long time. "You have to kill him!" she insisted. "You don't know what … what he did to me! And if you don't kill him for that, kill him because he'll be coming after you. Not for me but because Kelleren told him lies. Told him that you murdered people in Wild Horses."

"I know all about that."

"Then what are you standing there for?" she hissed in a fierce whisper, growing more agitated with each passing second. She tried to squirm out of the quilt, but Riler held it securely closed around her. Her efforts became violent. "God damn it, Lobo, if you won't do it let me! Let me kill the bastard!" Tears of frustration gleamed in her eyes.

"Shh! You don't want to do that, Rose."

"Yes, I DO!" she shouted, writhing violently, like a fish on a hook, under the quilt. "Let me GO, damn…."

Riler sighed. He didn't want to, but he punched her, not hard, but hard enough that she slumped into his arms, unconscious. He threw her limp form over his shoulder. He had wrapped three quarters of the quilt around her, leaving enough so that the rest would fall down around her head. Returning to the front room he peered out one of the windows that provided a good view of the parade ground. He saw no one stirring, and without hesitation he opened the door.

He crossed the parade ground with long strides, making for the spot where he had entered the fort. As he drew near he saw a knot of about a half dozen soldiers a hundred feet to his right, standing and talking in front of one of the barracks. They paid him no attention.

The guard who had spoken to him when he reached the top of the grade was still on duty. Riler gave him a curt nod in acknowledgement and started down the grade, keeping his chin tucked so that the brim of the forage cap concealed some of his face.

"Hold up there."

Riler stopped and turned. He surmised that there were more than a hundred soldiers in the garrison and he could only hope that this sentry didn't know each and every one of them well enough to realize, in the dark, that he didn't belong in an army-issue greatcoat. He sounded perturbed when he said, with a voice that was hoarse and slurred, as though he was drunk, "I'm following orders. Captain Telford's orders."

"What?" The sentry stepped closer. "What have you got there?" He reached out with his left hand — his Spencer carbine was in the right hand and tilted over his shoulder — and lifted the quilt enough to see Rose's tangled golden tresses. "What the hell…?"

"She's dead," said Riler curtly. "And I'm supposed to take the body out beyond the town a ways and leave it for the coyotes."

"He killed her," breathed the soldier. It wasn't a question. "He killed another one." He shook his head and let go of the quilt and took a step back. "That just ain't right."

"No it ain't," replied Riler. "And it ain't right that I have to do this."

"You should give her a Christian burial."

Riler turned and started down the steep grade.

* * *

By the time they got to the Cheyenne camp Riler could tell that Rose was conscious. At this hour most of the tent town was asleep, save for a few watering holes, so he was glad that Rose kept still and quiet, especially as he had expected some anger and outrage from her on the subject of his punching her.

All was quiet up at the fort, too, it seemed. At least there were no bugles blaring or bells ringing. Riler didn't expect Telford to be found until after daybreak, and by his reckoning, determined by the position of the moon in the sky, that gave them about six hours to clear out.

He was relieved to see Gus Freeman in the camp, and Freeman and Dohasan were just as relieved — and more than a little amazed — to see him. They were the only two stirring in the camp. The Cheyenne were in their skin lodges.

"You did it, Mister Riler!" exclaimed the Sioux youth. "I have to admit that I didn't think you had a chance."

"Praise the Lord you are both safe," exclaimed Gus, as Riler gently slid Rose off his shoulder and put her down on her feet. The quilt nearly slipped off her bare shoulders but she caught it and held it together at the neck and touched her swollen cheek gingerly.

"I had to do it, Rose," murmured Riler, as contrite as he had ever sounded in his whole life. "I needed you to pass for dead so as to get past the sentry."

"I could have pretended," she muttered. "I suppose Telford is still alive?"

Riler nodded.

"You should have killed him," she said, matter-of-factly. "Or let me. He knows about Wild Horses. Don't you understand? He's going to hunt you down for the glory of it. And he's going to hunt *me* down, too."

"He won't find you. I'm going to draw you a map to my place, and Gus is going to go with you to make sure you get there safe." He looked at the blacksmith, who nodded. Then he took a moment to study the expression on Rose Waldron's face. Rose was deep in thought, and looking very somber. She was silent for so long that he had to ask, "You want to go back to Julie and the Regret, is that it?"

She shook her head. "I wouldn't mind seeing Molly and Ana again, and especially Miss Julie. She was always looking out for me. She always put up with me. I didn't appreciate her until … until I was taken away. But no. I don't want to go back to the Regret. I'm done with all that. As God is my witness, I am. But then I don't expect God wants anything to do with me."

"That ain't true, Miss Rose," said Freeman. "'As far as the east is from the west, so far has He removed our transgressions from us.' Psalms 103. All you's gots to do is ask for forgiveness."

Rose glanced at the blacksmith and nodded, but she didn't look like she was buying it. Turning to Riler she said, "Why aren't you taking me?"

"I have unfinished business."

"Kelleren, you mean."

"That's right."

Incredulous, she shook her head. "You'll let Telford live but you're determined to see Kelleren dead? What chance do you have against him and all his men?"

"Well, there's only seven of them left. And Dohasan here is coming with me."

"Only seven!" Julie fumed, then grabbed Riler by the arm. "Please...please don't go. I don't want to…." Then she caught herself. To lose him? She chided herself. He wasn't hers to lose. He had made that clear enough that day at the Regret. He hadn't rescued her because he loved her, but rather because he was a man who wouldn't stand by and let bad things happen. She shook her head. "I don't want you to die." She turned her gaze to Dohasan. "Either one of you. Your father wouldn't want you to do this."

"I have to," said Dohasan. "I have to avenge my father. It is the Sioux way."

Rose just shook her head, but said no more.

A pile of wood stood nearby and Riler broke a branch off a dead limb, and used this to stir up the embers in the campfire until an orange glow illuminated the ground. Down on one knee he smoothed out the dirt and, with Gus and Rose looking on, drew the map, informing them of distance and direction and the time it would take to reach the several landmarks to look out for along the way.

When he was satisfied that the two understood he rose, used his foot to smooth out the dirt, obliterating the map. "You two better leave now. Go up the river like I showed you, then turn west, ride for an hour or two, rest until dawn and then keep moving. No one will find your tracks." He looked at Rose. "That captain will assume you headed back for Wild Horses on the Overland Trail. Just steer clear of the Overland and you should be fine."

Rose opened her mouth to speak, and Riler assumed she was going to try again to convince him to give up his vendetta with Kelleren and come with them. But, an expression of resignation on her face, she just shook her head, and walked to the buckskin.

"Hold up," said Riler and as she turned he took off his old leather belt and secured it around her slender waist to help hold the quilt closed. He had to tie it off, but the belt was limber from age. "I'll be wanting that back when I see you," he murmured.

She managed a brave smile, but it was clear by her expression that she didn't expect to see him ever again. He lifted her up into the saddle and collected the reins, gave them to her. Freeman saddled his horse and a moment later was mounted.

"I won't let you down, Lobo," he promised.

"You never have, Gus. Now get going."

The two rode out of the encampment with the horses at a walk. The wolfdog was on its feet and looking agitated. "Stay with me," said Riler quietly, knowing that the wolfdog was bothered by the departure of the buckskin. The command calmed the wolfdog. It sat on its haunches and watched Riler's face as the mountain man turned to Dohasan.

"Get your horse. We're leaving now."

CHAPTER 21

Three days later, Lobo Riler was laying on his belly at the crest of a low grassy rise on the eastern edge of the Sand Hills, drawing a bead on the head of the buffalo hunter Jim Early, who was himself laying on his belly at the crest of another, lower, grassy rise about a sixty yards further east. Beyond Early was a slow-moving sea of brown fur, a vast herd of buffalo moving slowly north, grazing on the new grass that had begun to turn the Sand Hills green.

It hadn't been difficult finding and following the trail of Kelleren's crew. Two wagons and a passel of horses left obvious marks on the prairie, which had yet to be baked and hardened by summer sun and wind. They had reached the North Platte night before last, crossed it in the morning, and with the Sand Hills in sight as yesterday's sun went down had seen the glow of the hide hunters' fires.

They had but one horse between them, and Riler had been in the saddle most of the time, at Dohasan's insistence. The Sioux lad had usually trotted alongside the sorrel that had once belonged to the man named Breck, sometimes holding on to the saddle when he tired, and

     JASON MANNING

when he was weary they rode double. Riler felt bad about hogging the horse but he knew Dohasan was right in stating that he was in no condition to walk long distances, much less run. Even so, long hours straddling a horse that was sometimes held to a walk but more often was allowed to trot wasn't very comfortable for someone who had been shot through with a .58 caliber Minie ball less than a fortnight ago.

Dohasan had thought to stock up on corn fritters and had acquired a second canteen back in the Laramie tent town, so they had food and water. Riler had downed a pronghorn on the second day out and they had cooked it and still carried some of the meat with them. It was the only shot — and the only fire — Riler had allowed, as they slowly but steadily gained ground on their prey. He assumed that if Kelleren was worried enough about him to spin that tall tale to Telford in hopes that the U.S. Army would take care of his problem, then he might still be watchful of his backtrail.

There was something else to be concerned about. The Plains Indians would be out hunting buffalo, too, now that winter was done, and these days most of the tribes harbored some measure of hostility towards the interloping white folks, be they hunters, trappers or pioneers. And regardless of their tribe, some young bucks out to prove themselves might jump at the chance to take a couple of scalps.

But they hadn't run into trouble of any sort, and now Riler was drawing a bead on the man who had nearly killed him back in Wild Horses. He was ready to settle accounts. He wasn't in a rage. He wasn't even angry. He was simply resolved to do a job that needed doing.

Next to Early was his reloader, who Riler identified as Jonah Johnson. Early probably had a second long gun, possibly another Springfield. Once Early fired a shot he would put the empty rifle down and take the loaded one from Johnson, who would reload the first. This would save the shooter precious seconds.

Maybe forty yards south of Early and Johnson were the two wagons and a cold campfire. Several saddle horses were tied to the wagons. That the crew had camped here led Riler to believe that the hide hunters had done some scouting and knew there was a herd coming their way, so they had hunkered down and waited for it. Riler recognized Kelleren and Sangre, the latter on the first wagon, as the black man, Morris, was with the second. They were ready to move the wagons out in a hurry if the herd turned towards the camp. Kelleren was standing on the slope of the low grassy rise, high enough to look over the rim and see the herd, and the mountain man had thoughts of shooting him first — until Kelleren was joined by Texas Jack, who carried two long guns, handing one to Kelleren, who then lay down and crawled up to the rim. It seemed that with Billy Heller dead, Kelleren had taken on the role of a shooter, with the ex-cowboy as his reloader. At that point, Early became the best target, and Riler decided it didn't really matter if Kelleren was the first to die.

He didn't plan on walking away with a single one of those men down there left alive.

Looking to his right, he saw Dohasan, belly-down like he was, gripping Seth Topper's sawed-off shotgun and peering through the grass on the rim of the rise with a fierce intensity that reminded Riler of a wolf on the hunt. That thought caused him to look over his left shoulder. The wolfdog was laying in the grass close by, head up, watching him intently. Riler smiled and murmured, "Stay with me" then turned his attention on Jim Early again.

Seconds later Early fired his Springfield. The hunter quickly put the rifle down and took the loaded one Johnson handed him. He was sighting on another buffalo when Riler squeezed the trigger of his Sharps. Before the smoke cleared he was reloading — breech block levered down, paper cartridge into the breech, shearing the paper off with the breech block and cocking the hammer. As he put his sight on Johnson he noticed Early hadn't moved. He was never going to move again. Riler heard Kelleren bellowing but didn't take his eye off his next target. Shocked, Johnson was staring at the dead hunter, and then turned his head to look around.

Riler put a bullet through Lazy Eye's skull and glanced to his right. He had told Dohasan to move when he fired the first shot and he caught a brief glimpse of the Indian youth's back as he loped away, on the backside of the rise, out of sight of the men below. Riler was keenly apprehensive — he had urged Dohasan to stay out of the fight, all the while knowing that the effort was pointless.

Keeping his head down, Riler reloaded the Sharps. Two men down. Five to go. The odds were better, but still stacked against him and Dohasan. More than one man down around the wagons was shooting at nothing, and he heard a bullet pass close enough to make a quick buzzing sound. He took a long deep breath to slow his heart and then raised his head, the Sharps' stock snug against his shoulder, and killed one of the lead mules in the wagon furthest away. He hated doing it, but he wanted his adversaries to worry about their livestock, especially the horses. The lead wagon was now immobilized, unless someone wanted to try to cut the dead mule out of the traces;

As he had hoped, someone yelled something about the horses, and Texas Jack appeared in a brave but foolhardy attempt to untie three sets of reins and then lead a trio of horses that had been unnerved by the shooting and the death of the mule just a few yards away. Once untied, two of them tried to rear back and free themselves, so that the ex-cowboy had to dig in his heels and lean back. Since he wasn't motionless, Riler aimed for the man's chest. The impact of the .52 caliber slug knocked him off his feet. Rein leather slipped from dying hands and the horses took off at the gallop.

By now the buffalo herd was moving. A few hundred of them — the portion of the herd closest to the shooting — were on the run, veering into the rest. It was like dominos falling, with the number that were moving steadily increasing, and with that the thunder of hundreds, and then thousands, of hooves rising in volume.

The Sharps reloaded, Riler surged to his feet, went over the crest of the hill and began running down the far slope, the Sharps held in his left hand, his right filled with the Colt Navy revolver. He couldn't see any of the remaining hide hunters at first but then one of them appeared going up the slope beyond the wagons. It was Morris, and Riler decided he was running away. Then he flinched as a bullet whined past his ear, and he saw the muzzle flash beneath the nearest wagon. He began shooting the Colt Navy on the run, aiming under the wagon, though he couldn't tell who the shooter was or if he had hit the man.

When Riler had fired six shots he holstered the empty Colt and threw himself to the ground, and none too soon. Another bullet whined right over his head, another muzzle flash visible beneath the wagon. Now he was less than forty yards away and he could see movement in the slanting shadow thrown by the wagon. Bringing his long gun to shoulder, he fired a shot, seeing a third muzzle flash simultaneously. This time the bullet plowed into the ground inches in front of him, flinging dirt into his face. He reloaded the Sharps again, expecting more bullets thrown his way. But there were none. He debated whether to get up and try to reach the wagons, but wondered if the man beneath the wagon was playing possum, waiting for him to stand.

Beyond the wagons he spotted Dohasan charging up the slope in pursuit of Morris. Then he saw the Sioux youth spin around, off balance, cutting loose with one barrel of buckshot from Seth Topper's old scattergun, shooting at someone on the far side of the wagons that Riler couldn't see. Then Dohasan went down and Riler surged to his feet and broke into a run. He glimpsed movement out of the corner of an eye and turned to see Chaytan crawling out from under the wagon, wobbling, clutching at the leg, bringing a pistol up to shoot at him. Riler saw something else — a streak of black and gray fur rushing down the slope and straight for the Indian hide hunter. As Riler stopped and swiveled, bringing the Sharps to his shoulder, Chaytan fired the pistol once, twice. The second bullet hit the mountain man in the leg and spoiled his aim — the .52 caliber slug from the Sharps smacked into the side of the wagon behind Chaytan, who was turning his pistol on the wolfdog, squeezing the trigger. The hammer fell on an empty chamber. The wolfdog leaped, a hundred of pounds of bone and sinew and bared fangs striking the hide hunter squarely and bearing him down. Chaytan was groping for the knife sheathed at his side when those fangs tore open his throat. In his death throes, the mute Sioux reloader stabbed the wolfdog once and then went limp, a geyser of bright red blood splashing the snarling face of his killer. The wolfdog savaged at the hide hunter's throat a few seconds more then collapsed on top of its prey.

Riler stumbled in that direction, a couple of agonizing steps. He

 Jason Manning

looked down at his leg. There was a growing stain of blood on his buckskin breeches at the thigh, but he could tell that no bone had been hit, and he surmised by the size of the bloodstain that no artery had been cut. Bent at the waist, he felt the back of his leg. The bullet had not passed through.

The unmistakable sound of the scattergun to his right made him look that way, just in time to see Kelleren on a mule that was going down. It was immediately obvious that he had cut the mule from the traces of the first wagon and was intending to flee, but Dohasan had killed the mule rather than Kelleren, whether by intent or because he was wounded and in pain, or because his target had been at the limit of the shotgun's range. Kelleren leaped free as the mule went down, landing clumsily, losing his balance, and falling. He got up and raised his pistol in Dohasan's direction.

"KELLEREN!" Riler's shout was hoarse and strident as he lurched in the direction of the hide-hunting crew's leader.

Kelleren spun around and dropped to one knee, the got up and began to hobble in Riler's direction, and Riler wasn't sure if he had been hurt when the mule went down or if he had taken some of Do-hasan's buckshot. Either way, the mountain man realized it was a boon. He dropped to one knee and began reloading the Sharps. The adrenaline was surging so strongly in him he hardly felt the throbbing pain in his leg. He focused solely on the process of reloading, glancing up once when he heard the telltale buzz of a bullet that didn't miss him by much. Kelleren was yelling now, but the thunder of the stampeding bison herd had become louder every minute and was loud enough now to drown him out. He was also brandishing a pistol, and fired a second time as he kept stumbling forward, then a third time. Riler felt a stinging sensation in his left right arm and looked to see that a bullet had torn through his buckskin shirt and grazed his upper arm.

Bringing the Sharps to his shoulder, he saw Kelleren aiming his pistol, not more than fifty feet away, but he kept moving forward and just when he pulled the trigger his bad leg gave out and he began to fall to the right. The shot went wide. Riler fired, but his target's sudden lurch to the right made him miss his mark. The slug hit Kelleren high in the left shoulder, spinning him around and he toppled, and began rolling down the hill. Riler hobbled hastily down the slope, and then *his* leg buckled and he fell forward and rolled on his shoulder, losing his grip on the empty Sharps, planting his feet and managing to push to his feet — in time to see Kelleren already on *his* feet, aiming the pistol at him, a grin on his stubbled, jowly face, his piggish eyes bright with anticipation.

"I'm gonna kill you, you sonuvabitch!" he crowed, and pulled the trigger.

The hammer fell on an empty chamber.

Kelleren stared at the pistol, outraged, and with a growl hurled it at Riler. He missed his mark, which outraged him even more, and his growl grew louder as he brandished a hunting knife. His rage gave him the strength and balance he needed to charge up the slope and Riler just had time to draw his own knife. Kelleren swung the knife laterally, trying to cut his foe, but Riler jumped back and barely evaded the blade. His left leg buckled and he fell. With a roar of elation, Kelleren lunged at him. Riler planted his right foot in the hide hunter's gut and with a grunt of exertion straightened that leg and used Kelleren's impetus to pitch him over his head. Kelleren landed poorly, and he writhed and wheezed in the tall grass long enough for Riler to push to his feet.

"Get up," growled Riler.

Kelleren groaned and rolled over onto hands and knees, lifted his head and looked at Riler and grinned. "I'm gonna take your scalp, Lobo. The last of the mountain men. Be a good trophy."

"Come and get it."

With a guttural snarl, Kelleren launched himself at Riler, staying low. Riler took a half-step forward with his right leg and planted it, pivoting, as Kelleren lashed out with his blade. Riler locked his left arm round the hide hunter's neck and fell backward, down-slope, and drove his knife to the hilt into Kelleren's back, the blade turned so that it glanced off the man's ribs. Ten inches of sharp steel plunged into Kelleren's body as the two men, locked in a deadly embrace, rolled

 JASON MANNING

down the slope a good thirty feet. When they came to a stop Riler pushed Kelleren's hefty, limp body off. It was willpower alone that got him to his feet.

"Damn you, Riler," rasped Kelleren. "You've killed me." He grinned, then coughed up a geyser of thick dark blood. His beady eyes widened, his mouth open wide, rivulets of blood running down his cheeks. Riler watched those eyes become glazed and sightless.

"Yeah," he gasped, swaying uncertainly on his feet. "Best thing I've ever done."

He looked over at the wolfdog draped over the body of Chaytan, and sighed. He managed to go up the slope to retrieve his Sharps and reloaded it before circling around behind the wagons. Dohasan lay up the grassy slope, unmoving, but Riler fought the urge to go to him.

There was one hide hunter unaccounted for.

He found Sangre. The Mexican teamster was sitting on the ground near the mules hitched to the second wagon. The front of his shirt was soaked with blood, and Riler concluded that this had been Dohasan's target when he turned and fired one barrel of the scattergun. As Riler approached, the Sharps at his shoulder and ready to shoot, Sangre looked up at him with an expression of resignation on his face. He nodded. "*A y me disparan, hombre.* Kill me."

"You've already been killed," replied Riler, and he leaned over to pick up the pistol that lay on the ground next to the Mexican, and tossed it away.

"*¿La mujer de pelo amarillo, ella está viva?*"

Riler nodded. "She's still alive."

"*Bueno, bueno....No les gustó lo que hicieron con ella.*"

Sangre's head fell forward and then his lifeless body slumped sideways as Riler heard the death rattle in the man's throat.

Riler limped up the slope to Dohasan, to have his worst fears realized. The Sioux youth was dead, sprawled on his back, Seth Topper's shotgun still in hand, looking up at the sky with sightless eyes.

Next, he checked on the wolfdog. To his surprise, the animal was alive. Chaytan's blade had struck just below the shoulder and apparently had missed the animal's lungs. Riler lay down with a groan in the grass splattered with the blood that had spewed from the Indian hide hunter's savaged throat, reached out to put his hand on the wolfdog.

"Stay with me," he breathed. "Stay with me."

Riler tore his homespun shirt into strips and after removing Chaytan's knife bound the wolfdog's wound. Only then did he get to his feet and limp past the wagons and up the next slope. The buffalo herd had passed, the thunder of their hooves dwindling. He found the remains of the hide hunter Morris nearby. The sign told Riler that the man had veered to the south but the stampeding herd was like a river that had jumped its banks, flowing in erratic patterns, and Morris had come too close. There wasn't much left of him, just a bloody pile of twisted limbs that no longer looked human.

Returning to the wolfdog, Riler sat down, cut open his deerskin breeches above the bullet wound in his left, and dug the slug out of his flesh before using what was left of his shirt to apply a tight dressing around the bleeding wound. Then he lay down and closed his eyes, reaching out to rest his hand on the wolfdog, which was still sprawled over the corpse of the man it had killed, breathing quick and shallow.

A buzzard awoke Riler when it landed on his chest. He swiped at it and it flew away. Up on his elbows, he looked around, and saw that other buzzards had already found the other bodies. There were at least a dozen on the ground, and more than that in the sky. Cursing, Riler got to his feet again, hobbled over to Dohasan's body and spent the rest of the day digging a grave for Seth Topper's adopted son, using his knife. He buried the scattergun with the Sioux lad.

Crawling under one of the wagons, he detached the large, steel pin that held the double-tree to the wagon tongue. It had a C-shaped iron attached to it which could serve as a wrench to loosen the retaining nuts from the axle prior to removing a wheel. This he used as a hammer to break the chains that held the wagon's tailgate in place, then scavenged some rope out of the wagon.

He left the tailgate and the rope near the wolfdog and walked to the sorrel horse that he and Dohasan had left about a hundred yards away. The horse had been unsaddled, then hobbled, and then tied to the saddle. Riler removed the hobbles, saddled the horse, and led him back to the wolfdog. Securing two long lengths of rope to one end of the tailgate, he gently moved the injured wolfdog onto the tailgate and secured it there with more rope.

"Let's go home," he murmured.

He lashed the other end of the two long ropes to the horn of his saddle. Mounting up, he headed west, dragging the wolfdog along on the makeshift travois.

EPILOGUE

Three weeks later, Julie Regret was in the kitchen preparing to make supper when she looked out the window and saw Lobo Riler riding into Wild Horses with Rose astride the saddle behind him. With a delighted gasp she rushed out of the kitchen and through the dining room and out onto the front porch just as Riler checked the tall buckskin in front of the Regret. Rose slid down off the horse and ran into Julie's open arms, weeping with joy. Julie had to fight back her own tears.

"Praise God you are alive and well!" she exclaimed, then smiled warmly as she touched the side of Rose's head. "Your hair is growing back."

"Yes. Praise God...and Lobo."

Julie held Rose at arm's length and drank in the sight of her. Rose wore a fringed buckskin dress belted at the waist. Noticing how Julie looked at it, she murmured, "This belonged to Lobo's Indian wife," she murmured, and glanced at the mountain man, who was smiling as he observed the reunion from his saddle. "I'll give it back to you," she said, and glanced at Julie. "I assume I still have some clothes here."

"Of course," said Julie.

"No need to give it back," said Riler.

"And what of your wolf?" asked Julie.

"I left him at the cabin. He's still healing up."

Julie stepped closer to the buckskin, put a hand on Riler's leg. "Gus showed up a week ago. Said you had made it home, all shot up again. Told me what happened to Dohasan."

Riler grimaced, nodding. "I tried to send Rose back with Gus but she wouldn't go. She looked out for me while I was mending."

Julie looked at Rose, back at Riler, and then away, nervously wiping hands that didn't need wiping on the apron she wore. She tried to keep a smile on her face to conceal how terribly alone she suddenly felt. She hadn't failed to notice that Rose was calling Riler by his other name now, and assumed that they would go as they had come — together. "Well, I thank you for bringing her all this way so I could see her."

Rose was studying Julie's expression and smiled pensively as she shook her head. "Not just to see you, Julie. I'm not going back with him."

"You're not?" Julie was startled. "How come? I thought…." She shrugged, suddenly self-conscious. "Well, I just assumed that you would stay with Mr. Riler."

Rose gazed up at the mountain man, smiling warmly. "I am very fond of this man. But, we're not in love." She looked earnestly at Julie. "And I *want* to be in love. Like you were with Moke. And like Lobo here was with his Cheyenne wife. So I've decided to go to San Francisco and make a new life for myself there."

Julie glanced behind her at the Regret. "That's just as well. Ana and Molly are gone. You see, I closed the brothel. After what happened here I just…I just couldn't continue. They headed to the town on the Laramie. I'm sure they'll be fine if they stick together."

"Any soldiers come around?" asked Riler, his gaze sweeping the quiet street.

"No. I was half-expecting them, though. Gus told me what happened at the fort." She touched Rose's face. "You poor girl. You've been through hell, haven't you?"

Rose shrugged. "It's all in the past. So I'm going to make a new like, Julie. I'm going to get honest work and maybe someday I'll meet a good man and fall in love and live happily ever after."

Julie grabbed her, hugged her tightly and began to weep, tears of happiness running down her cheeks.

Riler cleared his throat, feeling ill-at-ease all of a sudden. "I'm going to go down and see Gus. I think he might still have my pack mule. Reckon I'll go say goodbye to Seth, too, while I'm here. I'll be back." With that he kicked the buckskin into motion.

Julie watched him ride on down the street towards the blacksmith's forge on the other end of town. Rose watched Julie and smiled.

"You should go with him," she murmured.

"To see Gus?"

"No. When he goes back to the mountains you should go with him. He's lonely. So are you. And I've seen how you look at him."

Julie was flustered. "He doesn't want anything to do with me. I'm surprised he didn't want *you* to stay with him."

"Oh he wants me. So does every other man who sees me." Rose said it as a simple statement of fact, without even a hint of vanity "But that has nothing to do with love. It was my decision to leave, to go to San Francisco. I want to know what true love is like. You know. Lobo knows. And one day I will know."

Julie smiled warmly and touched Rose's face. "You're all grown up all of a sudden."

"Come on, let's get your things packed. Lobo will be back soon. You really should go with him, Julie. If you live in the past you're just not living."

Julie Regret smiled and took Rose by the hand. Together they went inside.